Great story! Compelling characters and situations. Mielke's talent as an author is only exceeded by his creative imagination."—*John Austin, Host of "Book Talk," WTAN Radio 1340 AM*

"A tremendous job in describing each character and scene. Fast paced action is never-ending. Blends well from one character or event to the other."—*Carol Hoyer, Ph.D., READER VIEWS*

"Original adventure. Use of humor successfully balances darker aspects of the plot."—*Christine DeZellar Tiedman, Editor, THE LIBRARY JOURNAL*

"Strong, well written. A fast-paced, exciting story."—*Tyler Tichelaar, Editor, READER VIEWS*

BOOKS by DAVID CARL MIELKE

<u>Novels</u>

The LENA MILLS TRILOGY
Mystic Sisters (2016)
A Nation Best Served Hot (2010)
Executive Deceit (2011)
--and—

THE SHARON RICHARDS SAGA
Nickelodium (2013)
Amerageddon (2014)

AUTOBIOGRAPHY
They Shoot Geezers, Don't They? (2016)

<u>GHOST WRITTEN AUTOBIOGRAPHIES</u>
My Name is Frank, I Come From Hell
Frank R. Eknif (2016)
Value Driven Success
Joe Garcia, CLU, ChFC (2016)

Please chack out the author's KICK

ASS Website:

davidcarlmielke.com

AMERAGEDDON

AMERICA'S WORST NIGHTMARE –
AND IT'S ONLY THE BEGINNING!

DAVID CARL MIELKE

AMERAGEDDON is a work of fiction. Though some characters, incidents and addresses are based on the historical record (see Acknowledgments at end of book), the work as a whole is a product of the author's imagination.

DC PRESS
P.O. Box 686
Sorrento, FL 32776
e-mail: dcpress1@yahoo.com
website: www.davidcarlmielke.com

Printed in the United States of America

COVER ART by

Graphic Design Services

www.michaelbydesign.com

AMERAGEDDON is based on current and past events, America's politically correct response to acts of terror, the constant threat of more attacks that could affect the stability of our homeland, and the growing number of disaffected U.S. citizens who pledge their allegiance to radical Islam.

This novel is dedicated to the courageous men and women of America's Armed Forces, who too often sacrifice life and limb in vain at the direction of feckless leaders more concerned with political expediency than protecting our country from ideologically driven harm.

The Author

"I always say my biggest worry is...an attack on a plane. It's a weapon of mass destruction in the hands of a terrorist and that includes a cyber-capability that trumps the defenses that we have." Robert Mueller, outgoing FBI Director, August 21, 2013

PROLOGUE

**INTERNATIONAL TERMINAL
JFK AIRPORT, NEW YORK
TUESDAY, 4 P.M.**

THE BEARDED ONE stood alone, scowling at anyone who dared invade his space. The team of nine stayed clear of their usually amicable crew chief, mistaking his anxious mood for anger. Chatting among themselves, they patiently waited for a "black-seal" customs agent to clear the Boeing 777-200 that had arrived from London Heathrow a half-hour earlier.

In two hours, the bearded one would cease to exist. Jabril Hosfani would shave off his bushy facial hair and flee to Canada under a new identity, leaving his family, friends and four decades of false pretenses behind. He felt no guilt about abandoning those he seemed to love. Eventually, he would be declared deceased. The company's group life insurance would have to suffice for his nagging, spendthrift wife and two spoiled teenage girls. Fending for themselves would be their penance to Allah.

Born in Michigan, Jabril was six when his mother and father perished in a multi-car accident. With no relatives willing to adopt the young child, he was raised in a Dearborn Islamic orphanage. His early education was divided between a local elementary school and a mosque, where he studied sharia law and memorized the Qur'an. Though a lifetime of Islamic teachings had thoroughly indoctrinated the young Muslim, he learned to mask his beliefs under the guise of consumer-driven goals, convincing everyone—his wife, children, friends and co-workers—that he was a patriotic American.

Nothing could be further from the truth.

Living with his family in Queens, New York, Jabril had worked for Air-Pro, the largest cleaning contractor at JFK International, for twenty-one years. More importantly, he had earned the trust of his company's management. As one of Air-Pro's crew chiefs, Jabril had a choice of work venues. For the last few months, he had cleaned flight decks. This last assignment would be no different.

Establishing precedence was part of the Plan.

Using Boeing graphic element mode control panel maps and sample switches, Jabril and two other carefully chosen crew chiefs had rehearsed their respective tasks countless times. Swiftness of execution was paramount, as were calculated responses to every contingency.

Unlike domestic flights with quick turn-around times, international flights had an average of two hours for customs inspection, refueling, catering and cleaning. After boarding and pre-flight checklists, Alpha Atlantic Airlines flight 2350 was due to depart at six p.m.

Lost in thought, the crew chief felt a tap on his shoulder. Lenny from the Bronx pointed to the "CLEARED" sign at the base of the stairs. Grabbing a black garbage bag, Jabril followed his crew up the stairs and into the cabin. Everyone carried cleaning agents, trash bags, as well as portable vacuum cleaners strapped to their backs.

Turning toward the cockpit, Jabril waved his hand at Lenny. "You take business," he ordered. "See you in a few."

Inside the flight deck, Jabril's apprehension disappeared. Turning on his vacuum to avoid suspicion, he closed the cockpit door and quickly proceeded with his nefarious task.

Three minutes later, Jabril switched off the vacuum and opened the door, relieved to see that no one had noticed his brief breach of protocol. To mask a slightly acrid odor, he sprayed Febreze throughout the cockpit. The entire episode had taken less than five minutes.

As his cleaners finished their assigned areas, each filled out a "sweep sheet," checking off their completed chores—seat cushions pulled up, back pockets inspected, galleys and lavatories cleaned—while noting anything suspicious. Before exiting the airplane, each worker handed Jabril his list. Anything amiss would delay departure and foil his segment of the Plan. He was relieved to see all the "comments" sections were blank.

Hiding his elation, Jabril descended the stairs and smiled at his friend.

"Everything okay, boss?" Lenny asked, concern written on his face.

"Must have been something I ate. I'm fine now. Thanks, Len." As Jabril walked away from his longtime associate for the last time, he waved. "Take care." Speed-dialing the only number on his burner phone, he left a one-word voice message: "Done."

Affixing a "Closed for Cleaning" sign outside and locking a nearby men's lavatory door, it took Jabril Hosfani about sixty minutes to morph into a smooth-faced Italian version of his former self. He even discarded his glasses for contact lenses.

Abandoning the family vehicle for a rental car registered under his new identity, Charles Mangione headed north toward the Canadian border. During the long, cross-country trip to Saskatchewan, he would keep his car radio on, waiting for news of the coordinated attacks. No matter the outcome, the former maintenance crew chief could be proud that he had performed his role flawlessly...for the glory of Allah.

1

GRADUATE CENTER
CITY UNIVERSITY OF NEW YORK
4 P.M.

DR. MUHAMMAD ABU MAZRA scanned the lecture hall and scowled. Thirty-four pairs of eyes stared back, impatiently waiting for the professor's talk on applied physics to end. The fifty-year-old professor smirked with disdain. *You are but ignorant lambs and I am your shepherd.*

"Read chapters twenty through twenty-four and be prepared to answer my questions at the next class," he ordered. "And remember, your final exam is in two weeks. You are dismissed."

The herd of disgruntled graduate students rushed for the exit. Whispered comments like "pontificating prick" and "smug bastard" filled the hallway. Small in stature, Dr. Abu Mazra was a giant in his field of physics. His resume was intimidating—Professor Emeritus of the CUNY Physics Department; author of seventeen textbooks on applied physics; an American Physics Society Fellowship; even a Nobel Prize.

Abu Mazra seemed to take pleasure in alienating everyone, subjecting fools and sycophants alike to his condescending attitude and gruff demeanor. The professor's essay exams were the most excruciating tests of mental acuity in any CUNY department. So rigorous were his standards, if he didn't grade on a curve, no one would pass.

The professor's focus turned inward as if he had flipped a mental switch. With a sigh, he closed his briefcase, strode offstage and walked slowly down the hallway to his office, a ten-by-ten cubicle that hardly befitted a man of his lofty credentials. Ignoring the stares and nods of recognition, he seemed to carry the weight of the world on his shoulders. Unlocking the office, he placed the briefcase on his desk and glanced at the digital clock above the door. *Four-fifteen! I'll be late.*

Hurrying to don his female disguise—a black burqa that covered everything but his eyes and hands—the professor hurried to his car. Despite the traffic, he managed to arrive at his Brooklyn mosque only five minutes late for the meeting with his imam, Mustafa Shabbah. A naturalized American citizen and disciple of Omar Abdel Rahman—the "Blind Sheikh"—Imam Shabbah was the only man on earth who could intimidate the learned professor. Abu Mazra was convinced that Allah himself could not exceed his spiritual leader's withering glare, should one be late for an appointment.

Also dressed in a burqa, the professor's protégé, Dr. Firouz Ahmed, was waiting anxiously by the mosque's side entrance. A thin man in his late twenties with a pencil mustache and serious, penetrating eyes, American-born Ahmed was the most brilliant of Abu Mazra's former students. He was a conceptual thinker who had developed software to hack into an airplane's communications, address

12

and reporting system—"ACARS," including automatic detection protocol, commonly referred to as "pings." Using the relatively new SARH bistatic technology, Ahmed had also devised a complex method to remotely capture control of and re-route an airliner during flight. This practice was commonly called "spoofing." His theories were sound but had only been tested harmlessly on boats and smaller aircraft.

Good fortune blessed the learned professor this day, for the imam had more weighty matters on his mind than tardiness. Beckoning both men with a wave, Shabbah led them to a deserted corner of the mosque. "Have you received confirmation? Is everyone in place?"

"Yes, imam," replied the professor. Ahmed nodded in agreement.

In addition to technological development, Ahmed was the communication liaison between the professor and the teams of martyrs. "Do not speak unless spoken to directly," Abu Mazra had warned Ahmed before the meeting. "You are but my assistant and mean nothing to the imam." Looking none too pleased, Ahmed acknowledged the instruction with a frown.

Eager for news but careful to avoid specifics, Imam Shabbah was well aware that his mosque was on Homeland Security's "Watch List." Parabolic microphones could be intercepting their conversation from outside. Frequent sweeps inside his temple had often revealed hidden bugs left by adversarial interlopers.

Financed by shadowy Islamic charitable organizations in the Middle East and America, the imam had access to nearly unlimited funds for his terrorist endeavors. Shabbah had spent the money freely over the last decade recruiting and organizing militant jihadists into teams, each with the goal of mass destruction. The esteemed Professor Abu Mazra, using his status as a Nobel Prize recipient to ward off any suspicion, was the imam's training and logistics coordinator.

"And what of the principals?" the imam asked. "Principals" was code for airplanes.

"All are on schedule and prepared," the professor answered. "There are no delays and all the conditions are ideal, *Insha'Allah.*"

"*Insha'Allah,*" echoed the imam, looking upward with raised arms. Laying a hand on Abu Mazra's shoulder, Shabbah added, "We will only get one chance at this before countermeasures are taken. Muhammad, my son, if Allah blesses us this day, your name will live forever."

Other than his wife, no one had addressed the professor by his given name in years. The imam's hand on one's shoulder was the ultimate sign of respect. Kneeling in obeisance, Abu Mazra bowed his head and gushed, "I am but an instrument of Almighty Allah. The Plan is in His hands."

Fearing that they had been talking too loudly, the imam put a finger to his lips and whispered, "We must pray for His blessing. *Allahu Akbar. Alhamdulillah.* Allah is great. Glory be to Allah."

Shabbah concluded with a wave of his hand.

Firouz Ahmed followed Abu Mazra out of the mosque at a respectful distance. Before, during, and after the meeting, the young genius had remained silent. Six words from the mouth of his mentor had stuck in Ahmed's mind like thorns, festering resentment. *"You mean nothing to the imam."*

Dismissing the young protégé with a curt nod, the professor walked to his car, exalting in the imam's praise. A feeling of divine grace had replaced his exhaustion. Abu Mazra sat behind the steering wheel and rocked silently in prayer, repeating the mantra in his mind. *Insha'Allah, insha'Allah...*

Before entering his own car, Firouz Ahmed stared at the older man. Seething in anger, he mumbled to himself, "You pompous asshole! I've done all the work and you get all the credit."

After two years of planning, preparations were complete. Every action had been clothed in deception. Timing was everything. If the three aircraft departed their respective gates on schedule, a team of martyrs would execute a series of coordinated attacks that would far exceed the casualties of 9-11, destroy the airline industry, cripple the nation's economy and bring the "Great Satan" to its knees.

2

GREATER PHILADELPHIA

THOSE WHO believe that luck has nothing to do with financial success have never met someone like Duncan Richards.

In the early 1960s, Seamus and Sadie Richards wanted children but, for medical reasons, could not produce their own. So they adopted Duncan and his older brother Francis, infants from two different birth mothers. The hard-working, second-generation Irish immigrants dutifully raised their sons in middle-class Havertown, Pennsylvania, a western suburb of Philadelphia.

Francis—named by Sadie after her favorite crooner, Francis Albert Sinatra—was the elder sibling by a year. Duncan was named by Seamus, who for no logical reason thought the name sounded regal. During their formative years, both boys quarreled constantly and grew painfully familiar with the terms "grounded" and "time out." Deceptively charming and demonstrative, Francis—called Frankie by everyone except his mother—took shortcuts whenever possible and delighted in bullying his younger sibling. Intelligent, patient and thoughtful, Duncan always found ways to get even.

Upon graduation from Havertown High School, Frankie turned down his father's offer to join the family salvage business in favor of an apprenticeship with a shady coin dealer, where the impatient youngster learned that knowledge gave him a license to steal, and profit was earned by cheating others.

In contrast, Duncan eagerly accepted a role in his father's company, where he learned that, in the long run, a reputation for honesty and fair dealing was worth more than immediate gain. Though Seamus ran a successful business, Duncan convinced him to bid more aggressively on projects and buy large ads in the Philadelphia area Yellow Pages. The charismatic young man was soon seen on local TV stations with entertaining ads and a signature phrase, "Before You Wreck It, Let Us Check It." A year after Duncan joined Richards Salvage, it was the leading company of its kind in Eastern Pennsylvania.

Seamus Richards had one bad habit. He was a heavy smoker, which led to his demise from lung cancer at an early age. Duncan inherited the business, changed its name to "Richards Wreck and Roll," and was well on his way toward financial security by his mid-twenties.

While brash Frankie gained weight and had shallow affairs, lean and tall Duncan "went steady" with one girl throughout high school, Sharon Ainsworth—a beautiful physical fitness fanatic and dedicated student.

After graduation, Sharon stubbornly put Duncan's marriage proposals on hold. Her 4.6 grade average in high school bought a full scholarship in pre-law at nearby Drexel University. A natural at languages, she studied French,

Arabic, Farsi, Persian and Turkish. After seven years, Sharon had become reasonably fluent in many of the most common Middle-Eastern dialects, all the while earning black belts in both judo and karate.

Driven by laser-like goals and an urge to succeed that amazed her instructors, she earned a JD in criminal forensics in record time. Rejecting offers of immediate employment with local law firms, Sharon, now age twenty-five, applied for and was immediately accepted into the FBI's Tactical Recruiting Program.

After basic training at Quantico, Virginia, she was assigned to the DC headquarters as a counter-terrorism analyst. Because of her knowledge of Middle-Eastern languages, Sharon was also tasked to liaise with the NSA in foreign and domestic surveillance. Over the next few years, she and the FBI's team of agents intervened and prevented over five hundred potential terrorist incidents, foreign and domestic.

By the early 1990s, Duncan had run out of patience. Traveling to her apartment in Washington with a ring in one pocket and a "Dear Jane" letter in the other, he was determined to give Sharon an ultimatum. She preempted him with the news of her promotion and transfer as Deputy Director of the Philadelphia FBI Regional Office.

"They say I'm one of their 'rising stars' and can write my own ticket," she gloated, proud of her well-earned success. "I'm ready now, lover if you'll still have me."

Nine years after their wedding, Sharon gave birth to twin boys. By the second decade of the twenty-first century, Duncan, Sharon, Dougie and Damon were the prototypical

"Generation X" family of four—healthy, happy and financially sound.

One summer day, Duncan successfully bid on the contents of an old house in Merion, outside of Philadelphia. Rummaging for valuable items before the old Victorian was demolished, he found a small tin box in the attic. Inside the box were a number of old nickels, all dated 1913. Curious to see if they were worth any more than face value, Duncan brought one of the coins to his brother. Trusting Frankie's numismatic expertise but hardly his business ethics, Duncan neglected to mention the others he had found.

Frankie was beside himself with excitement when he saw the date on the nickel. "Bro, remember the nickel that sold at auction for over three million dollars a while ago?"

"You know I don't keep up with the news unless it affects me or my..."

"It was a Liberty-head or 'V' nickel, dated 1913," Frankie interrupted. "Only five are known to exist, and this coin is another one, or it's the best-goddamned fake I've ever seen!"

Struggling to keep his composure, he continued, "Over the last hundred years, there have been lots of attempts to fake these coins. This one looks to be nearly flawless. The only way to find out if it's real is to have it authenticated by experts. Let's send this off to NGC, the Numismatic Guaranty Corporation. If it's genuine, I'll have them grade it. And if I'm right, bro, you're gonna be rich—very rich!" Conjuring up his most pitiful expression, Frankie added, "Sure hope you'll share the wealth with your poor brother."

In a short while, the coin came back certified as authentic. Frankie was right. The nickel graded better than the other five known copies, making it "unique." At auction, Duncan's coin sold for over eight million dollars.

Frankie's agreed share was ten percent, most of which he predictably spent on booze and women. Unlike his profligate brother, Duncan had other plans. In addition to the financial windfall, he was an instant celebrity. Invited to tell his story at the next American Numismatic Association convention as well as on national talk shows, the former television huckster was in his element, cracking one-liners and charming the viewers.

Full of himself, Duncan impulsively revealed another 1913 nickel on the *Late Show with David Letterman*, incurring the wrath of collectors, charges of fraud and public ridicule. With any rare collectible, speculation of an unknown quantity poisons the market value of all similar specimens, let alone one of the world's most celebrated coins. How many more did he have? And how would the anonymous buyer of the sixth coin react, having paid for a "unique" 1913 Liberty-head nickel?

Frankie's grisly murder answered the last question. Devastated and in fear for his family's safety, Duncan's grief turned to thoughts of revenge. Using Sharon's FBI resources, he created a plan which led to the death of the assassin and his sponsor, the anonymous buyer—both international criminals.

Hailed as a hero and once again a media darling, Duncan Richards was in for an even greater shock. Less than a year later, he learned through a DNA match that he was the sole recipient of a $150 million trust fund.

But good fortune is a fickle mistress. Duncan's luck was about to run out.

Hearing a car horn, Sharon Richards glanced at her watch— one p.m. "Boys, get a move on!" she shouted up the stairway. "Our ride's here."

Muttering typical teenage complaints and with iPad buds firmly jammed into their ears, Dougie and Damon trundled down the stairs, each toting a large suitcase.

"This trip better be worth it," groused Damon between chomps on his chewing gum.

"If we're so rich, why can't we hire somebody to lug this shit?" Dougie complained, following his brother's lead.

"Watch your mouths," snapped Duncan, glaring at his sons. The obscene wealth he had inherited months ago came with a cloud of ever-present guilt that fed at his psyche like a parasite. Holding open the front door of their two-story home in Chestnut Hill, a northwest suburb of Philadelphia, he added, "Don't you dare say anything like that in public."

Chastened, both boys lugged their bags down the driveway in silence. Handing the luggage over to the driver with a polite "thank you," they piled into the rented limousine and waited mutely for their parents, who were traveling with four large pieces of luggage and two carry-ons.

Duncan and Sharon were strict parents, putting up a united front with their boys, especially when it came to manners. Their father had a short temper, particularly of late. But Dad wasn't the parent they feared. Mom was a former FBI agent with two black belts in the martial arts. She wouldn't dream of using her martial skills on the twins, but her aura of command was intimidating. One stern look from the "Mominator" was enough to bring any thoughts of teenage rebellion to an abrupt halt.

Dad was the extrovert in the family. Appearing frequently on television, Duncan's humorous and irreverent banter, coupled with the sensational events of his recent past, made him popular with television talk show hosts.

Recognized frequently in public, Duncan's celebrity had yet to attract the attention of the paparazzi, much to Sharon's relief. Usually quiet and reserved, she kept most opinions to herself. Duncan and Sharon had been soul mates since high school and loved each other unconditionally. As long as it didn't interfere with her career, she took his fame in stride.

Duncan's sudden inherited wealth was more of a challenge. Both took pains to keep the windfall a secret, but the sudden fortune was both a blessing and a curse. Sharon was grateful for the blessing but determined to keep the latter from destroying her family.

Relishing her role as "critic-in-chief," Sharon didn't hesitate to bring Duncan down to earth whenever he got a little too full of himself. Addressing her husband as "Donut"—a childhood nickname bestowed by his brother Frankie—was her signal that he had crossed the line from humorous to obnoxious.

Lately, however, the burden of wealth had taken its toll. Duncan would sit at his computer for hours brooding over his assets, knowing full well that he had relegated management of his wealth to a law firm's trust department. Over his initial objection, Sharon had booked an "owner's suite" on a fifteen-day Caribbean cruise, hoping that privacy, pampered luxury and a daily dose of love-making would make her darling husband relax and reconnect with the important things in life.

"Come on dear, don't be such a Gloomy Gus," she said on the two-hour drive to the Manhattan Cruise Terminal. Caressing Duncan's hand suggestively, she whispered in his ear, "I'm going to ravish your bod, you big stud." That brought a grin to Duncan's face.

"Ooo...is someone rising to the occasion?" Sharon added, sliding her hand south.

"Not in front of the boys," he complained, removing her probing fingers from his upper thigh.

Sharon changed her focus. Face the twins, she addressed the two fourteen-year-olds like a rabble-rousing scout leader at summer camp. "Just think of all the fab food and fun we're going to have. Right, guys?"

Battling hoards of ancient Gorgons, Dougie was glued to his iPad and ignored the question. Damon looked up from texting his friends. "Huh? Oh, yeah...I guess."

"You can do better than that," she coaxed. "How about a chorus of 'Ninety-nine bottles of beer on the wall?'"

Both boys looked at their mother and groaned. Had she suddenly turned into a space alien?

"Isn't this limousine a bit ostentatious?" Duncan asked, trying to bring his wife back to earth. In spite of their wealth, Sharon was habitually frugal. She had compared the cost of long-term parking their new Range Rover for fifteen days against the round trip limo fee to the Manhattan Cruise

Terminal. In addition, she argued, there would be less hassle at the terminal and they wouldn't have to worry about their vehicle being vandalized or stolen.

"Trust me, darling. This costs less. Besides, we got it. Let's enjoy it."

He laughed. "Since when did you turn into a Jewish American Princess?"

"You forget, Mr. Donut, I was an FBI analyst."

"How do you spell that?" Duncan replied, tweaking her ego with a sarcastic smile.

Sharon punched him hard in the shoulder, eliciting a cry of pain. "You're not my Donut today. You're the hole."

Damon looked up from his phone. "Now children. No fighting in the car."

All five, including the driver, broke up in laughter.

At Pier 88, the limo was searched twice by security agents before being allowed to proceed toward the loading area. At 150,000 tons and sporting twenty decks, the *Magnificence of the Seas* was currently the largest cruise ship in the world. So deep was its draft, only a handful of ports around the world could accommodate the behemoth's docking requirements. Boasting twenty-three restaurants, ten different entertainment venues and a myriad of amenities designed to accommodate the ship's 6,000 passengers and crew, the floating fun ship was on schedule to depart in three hours for its round trip to Nassau, St. Thomas and five other Caribbean islands.

Duncan, Sharon and the twins got out of the limo, craned their necks upward and gasped. "I knew the ship was big, but this is ridiculous!" Sharon exclaimed. "The brochure doesn't do it justice."

"We're gonna get lost," Duncan added.

Sarcastic Damon couldn't resist mimicking his mother's earlier pep talk. "Nah, just think of all the fab food and fun we're going to have!"

"And babes," added Dougie, poking his mom in the ribs. "This thing's gonna have zillions of babes!"

"I'll babe you!" Sharon snorted, grabbing her wise-ass son and tickling him.

Duncan broke up the fun. "Hey, enough horsing around! Our driver will take care of the luggage. I've got your passports and tickets ready. Now march!" He pointed to a sign that read, "Preferred Boarding."

Once registered, they followed a smiling porter onto an elevator that took them to the fourteenth floor. Down the corridor toward the front of the ship, they entered their two-story starboard-facing suite and were introduced to Manuel, the family's personal butler for the duration of the cruise.

Dougie gawked at the glamorous furnishings. Pointing to the spacious balcony with its own Jacuzzi, he asked, "Is this all ours?"

"Yes, it is," Manuel replied, "and you boys also have this...," he said, opening a door to a connecting room with its own balcony, "all to yourselves."

"Awesome!" exclaimed Damon.

"Sick!" echoed Dougie.

"Who's sick?" asked Duncan, alarmed. "You better not be coming down..."

"Dad, get with the program," Damon interrupted. "It's the latest term we use, like you *old people* say 'cool' or 'far out.'"

Sharon laughed and joined in. "Or *ancient* Mom Sadie used to say, 'the bee's knees' or 'the cat's meow.'"

During the family wordplay, Manuel stood patiently aside, expressionless. Seeing an opening, he explained all the features of the suites and how they worked. The butler ended with, "Is there anything I can get for you before we sail?"

"Yeah, food. I'm starved," Damon answered immediately.

"Babes!" Dougie echoed, stifling a giggle upon seeing his mother's look of disapproval.

Manuel had a son of his own about the boys' age. Smiling, he had a ready answer. "While I retrieve your luggage, may I suggest dining on the foredeck three floors up? There's a buffet waiting for you...and I'm sure plenty of...babes...as well."

He produced four deck maps and gave one to each of his charges. "Most young people like to explore the ship before we sail. You probably think you're going to get lost, but you'll find your way around in no time, I assure you."

"Let's do what the man says," Sharon suggested. "I'm hungry too."

Seeing his boys this excited, Duncan hugged Sharon and chuckled. "Looks like you hit a 'sick' home run...babe."

3

PIER 88
MANHATTAN CRUISE TERMINAL

TWENTY MINUTES after the Richards family arrived, six Saudi nationals drove up in a powder-blue stretch limousine. Leaving the driver to check in a small mountain of luggage, two imposing bodyguards escorted one male and two females to the same "Preferred Boarding" queue, where they registered for the fifteen-day Caribbean cruise.

Surrendering their Saudi passports, the three passengers paused briefly for an inspection of their one carry-on item, a large case with a Toshiba laptop and an odd-looking camera with a tripod. "The latest in technology," explained the young Saudi male.

The three passengers were escorted by a fawning cruise line executive aboard the massive ocean liner to a midship elevator, where they ascended three floors, walked a short way down the wide corridor and entered a Royal Suite, one of the most expensive rooms on the port side.

Only the best would do for a prince of the Saudi royal family and two of his wives. In truth, the three Saudis were look-alike imposters, extensively rehearsed in royal mannerisms and fluent in English, Arabic and Farsi. Their Saudi passports had been cloned from originals by the latest 3-D technology. Based upon their close resemblance to the passport images, each was waved through security without question. Oblivious to the mission's purpose, the two "wives" had been told that they were simply going on a cruise with a handsome escort. Both were instructed to obey their dashing leader and keep their mouths shut.

Raised in Saudi Arabia under strict Wahhabi principles, the male had trained with al-Qaeda leadership in the mountains of Waziristan, attended U.S. schools under a student visa and, after graduation, used forged identification to integrate anonymously into American society. Now twenty, the young jihadist had joined a Brooklyn mosque where he kept a low profile, prayed to Allah and trained for this mission with the computer genius, Dr. Firouz Ahmed.

So efficient was the ship's concierge staff that the three passengers found their luggage in the suite when they arrived. Abruptly dismissing the room's assigned butler, the fraudulent Saudi national switched on the "Do Not Disturb" sign, locked the entrance door and fell to his well-rehearsed preparations.

The Plan was simple in concept, complex in execution. After September 11, 2001, the western world had shuddered to a pause. With the Plan's three coordinated attacks, it would freeze to a halt.

Over a decade had passed since that September day of reckoning. The United States had wasted thousands of lives and billions of dollars on futile campaigns of vengeance and nation-building in Iraq, Afghanistan and throughout the Moslem world. After playing cat-and-mouse with weapons inspectors for years, Iran was at last nuclear-capable, arrogantly disseminating dirty bombs to proxy terrorists and daring the world to interfere with its goal of regional domination. All the while, the rogue nation continued to perfect the marriage of its nuclear warheads with medium- and long-range missiles.

Israel, America's prickly ally, was striking out in limited air attacks. Surrounded by countries dominated by radical Muslim factions, the Jewish state was poised to defend itself, yet had not taken that final step toward regional annihilation.

Since the Prophet Muhammad died in the year 632 A.D., conflict between the Sunni, Shiite and other sects had been a fact of life. Whichever faction held the most power dominated the others without mercy. The practitioners of radical Islam—between ten and twenty percent of the three billion Muslims in the world—controlled the remaining peace-loving moderates through intimidation and violence. The way of the past was still the way of the present.

In December 1941, the Japanese Empire launched a sneak attack on Pearl Harbor, waking the previously neutral "Sleeping Giant." With single-minded purpose, the United States of America rallied behind its leaders and forged a two-front assault on the Axis powers, led by Japan and Germany. Four years of devastating retaliation had led to a victorious end of the "Good War" and the beginning of America's unprecedented prosperity. But since the mid-sixties, political polarization and liberal guilt had slowly eroded America's dominance, leaving the leader of the free world a confused shell of its former self.

"Al-Qaeda is on the run," boasted a naïve American president, thinking that his golden oratory, the death of Osama bin Laden and a few drone strikes would make it so.

Its enemies knew better. America was still vulnerable. After this day, there would be no doubt.

Ibrahim al Rafjani, alias Muhammad bin Fahd—third generation cousin to Saudi Arabia's King Abdullah bin Abdulaziz—carefully unpacked the computer case while his two beautiful consorts cavorted naked in the Jacuzzi, outside on their private balcony. The women beckoned him to join in their frivolity. Though he felt a stirring in his loins, Rafi—his American nickname—dismissed the two with a wave of his hand. There would be plenty of time before the ship sailed to satisfy his libido. Duty took precedence.

Rafi removed the Toshiba laptop from its case. Booting up the computer, he tested the viability of its only application created by Dr. Firouz Ahmed, a student of the renowned Professor Abu Mazra. Satisfied that all was in order, Rafi shut down the computer, carefully returned it to its place, locked the case and deposited it in a corner of the suite's large clothes closet.

With an hour or more to kill before the mandatory lifeboat drill, he removed his clothes and joined his two lovely accomplices in the hot tub for an extended session of debauchery. Given the magnitude of his assignment and sacrifice, surely Allah would forgive this one final indiscretion.

Later, basking in the glow of sexual release, Rafi instructed his companions to dress in western garb. "Before the ship is underway, there will be an emergency lifeboat drill," he explained. "Say nothing to anyone. After the drill, we must return to our suite immediately. There will be no exploring the ship before or after the drill, understand?"

Both women nodded respectfully.

Returning to the balcony alone, Rafi looked over the railing to observe the ground crew's preparation for departure. Then, leaning back in a lounge chair, he reflected on the outcome of his single-minded mission. *Today the "Great Satan" will tremble under Your wrath. Insha'Allah.*

Looking upward at the nearly cloudless sky, he placed both hands behind his head and smiled. *"This is a good day to die."*

4

INTERNATIONAL TERMINAL
JFK AIRPORT
5:45 P.M.

AFTER COMPLETING his walk-around, Captain Andrew Nelson climbed the forward stairs and entered the cockpit of his Boeing 777-200. Sitting in the right seat was a familiar face—Patrick Boynton, the co-pilot for this trip.

"How's the family?" Nelson asked, shaking Boynton's hand.

"Fine, Cap. And yours?"

Taking the captain's seat, the fifty-nine-year-old pilot sighed. "The last kid has finally flown the coop. Amy's good, but I can tell she's not looking forward to having me home on a permanent basis." In one week, the former Navy commander and senior Alpha Atlantic pilot would turn sixty and face mandatory retirement.

"I sympathize with you. Karen's the boss at my house too. What are your plans?"

"Plans? Grow old and drive my wife crazy, I guess," Nelson answered. "Got no hobbies, hate golf and politics, been everywhere. I'm only good at one thing—flying these giant people-pushers. Maybe I'll write a memoir and call it 'One-Trick Pony.'"

Boynton laughed. "Jeez, Cap, you make retirement sound depressing."

"They say it beats the alternative," Nelson added. Removing an iPad from his briefcase, he loaded the preset flight plan. "Let's do it. All charts?"

"On board," answered Boynton.

"Flight plan?"

"Loaded."

"Weight and balance?"

"Verified."

"V speed? Flaps?"

"Calculated and entered."

"Parking brakes?"

"On."

"Start the ACARS."

"ACARS connected and started..."

Completing the remaining gate checks with his co-pilot, Nelson briefed the crew and verified that all doors were secured and jetways retracted. Then he ran through the engine checklist.

Andrew switched on the cabin speakers. "This is Captain Nelson. I'll be your pilot today. Assisting me is First Officer Boynton. Today's flight on the triple seven will take us over the North Pole, non-stop to Amsterdam Schiphol Airport. The weather looks good and a brisk tailwind should help us arrive in a little less than the scheduled six hours, forty-five minutes, approximately eight a.m. local time.

"Please sit back and enjoy the trip...and thank you for choosing Alpha Atlantic Airlines." Nelson switched off the internal intercom and called the tower.

"Ground control, Triple-A 2350. Clear to push back?"

"Triple-A 2350. You are clear."

Nelson glanced at Boynton. "Clear to start," he announced. "Throttle power levers?"

"Idle."

"Engine area?"

"Clear..."

Once the engines were started, Nelson requested permission to taxi.

"Triple-A 2350, cleared for pushback, tail right," was the response. "Taxi to 31-Left."

Five minutes later, the airplane reached its designated runway. Third in line, Nelson and Boynton went through the pre-takeoff checklist. The co-pilot noticed a slight resistance when cycling the autopilot switch, but verified "off" and continued with the list.

As the last plane ahead roared into the sky, Nelson positioned his 777 just short of the runway and keyed the tower. "Triple-A 2350. Request clearance for takeoff."

"Triple-A 2350, you are clear for takeoff."

"Attendants, secure for departure," the captain alerted the cabin stewards. While turning onto the runway, Nelson gave the crew twenty seconds to buckle-up before pushing the chime button twice, releasing the brakes and easing the throttle forward. As the airplane gathered speed and reached V1—the point of no return—the captain glanced at the clock. It read 6:21 p.m. local time.

5

ONE HOUR EARLIER

ON BOARD the *Magnificence*, the Richards family returned to the suite and tossed their orange flotation vests onto the master bed. With the mandatory lifeboat drill completed, the ship had departed its dock. The boys were eager to ditch their boring parents for a teen activity orientation scheduled for 5:45 p.m.

"Want to join them?" Duncan asked his wife with a grin, teasing a groan of protest from the twins.

"We wouldn't want to cramp their style, dear, especially if they're cruisin' for babes."

The boys took this as permission to leave and scrambled toward the door. "Hey, wait a minute!" she barked. "You both have watches. Be back to your room next door by seven-thirty. We're scheduled for supper at eight. Don't be late. That's an order!"

The boys nodded and raced toward freedom. Duncan laughed. "Not excited at all, are they?"

Sharon ignored the comment. Handing him her deck map, she said, "Why don't you go check out the restaurants and find one for tonight. Or better yet," she added, heading for the suite's large balcony, "you can stay here with me as we pass by the Statue of Liberty."

Duncan followed her to the balcony. The ship had passed Ellis Island and was approaching the statue. Sharon marveled at America's most famous icon. "Isn't she beautiful?"

Duncan wrapped his arms around her. "Yes, you are," he answered with a lingering kiss.

"Flattery will get you everywhere, Lover Boy," she answered, caressing his bulge.

"Careful, there's a lady watching," he whispered, pointing to the statue. "We've got lots of time. Let's wait until we're in the Atlantic." Relaxing their embrace, they passed by the statue, silently admiring Lady Liberty's graceful elegance.

Sharon looked in Duncan's eyes and broke the silence. "Do you know how lucky we are? And I don't mean the money," she added. "We're healthy, we've got two great children and, after all these years, our marriage couldn't be stronger."

Duncan looked away toward the west shore of the Hudson River.

"What's the matter, darling?" she asked, snuggling her head against his chest.

"I've loved you ever since grade school," he murmured. "You've been my rock and all I've ever been to you is a selfish pain in the ass."

Sharon turned his head back toward her and smiled. "But you're *my* pain in the ass. And you're not selfish. You're loyal, a great father to our kids..."

"I'm glad you did this," he interrupted.

"Did what?"

"This cruise. It's been hectic these past few months. We needed to slow down and recharge." He sighed and sat back on a large deck chair, beckoning her to join him.

Finally, thought Sharon as she snuggled against him on the chair, *my Donut has come back to me.*

6

IBRAHIM AL RAFJANI looked at his watch. It read 5:37 p.m. After the lifeboat drill, he and his two beautiful companions had returned to their suite, where the women began changing clothes for the first seating. Grabbing his large case, Rafi headed for the balcony. "Don't bother changing," he ordered, shaking his head. "We will call for room service later. Now go watch television or read something. Until I summon you, I want to be left alone on the balcony, understand?"

The women looked disappointed but nodded silently in submission. Rafi glared at his companions to emphasize the seriousness of his order, then closed the curtains and slid the door closed behind him. Opening the large case, he began removing its contents, placing everything neatly on the balcony deck chairs. Putting aside the Toshiba Qosimo laptop, he extracted sections of a long-range antenna and its tripod that were cleverly designed as a frame surrounding the computer. After assembling the antenna, using a USB cable, he connected the "camera"—actually a SARH automatic line-of-sight guidance system—to the antenna, and it to an electronic signal booster. Plugging the booster cord into a balcony outlet, he placed both the laptop and assembled antenna system on top of a small table anchored to the deck.

With the daunting task at hand, Rafi had not been paying attention to the ship's progress through Lower Hudson River. Craning his neck to his left, he saw the Statue of Liberty receding in the distance. "Great Satan's whore," Imam Shabbah had called the statue during one of his fervent rants.

Placing the laptop and antenna atop a second balcony table, Rafi booted up the computer. He aimed the antenna toward the sky and the general path his target would take. Since there were only two optional programs on the hard drive, the computer sprang to life almost immediately, displaying only a few icons on its desktop. Clicking on "OOOI," he saw that the target had departed its gate but was still on the ground. His watch read 6:10, within the Plan's parameter, given the distance from gate to the runway. *Let there be a short line for takeoff.*

Rafi felt flush with anticipation and checked his pulse. *Over a hundred beats per minute!* The consequences of the impending task weighed on his mind like an anvil. Waiting was agonizing. To ease his anxiety, he looked to his left and fixated on the receding lower tip of Manhattan and the new 9-11 Memorial Tower, scene of Allah's most demoralizing victory. *After today, this symbol of American resurrection will mean nothing!*

Consumed with worry, Rafi sat down and began rocking back and forth, watching the computer screen and softly chanting, "*Insha'Allah, Insha'Allah, Insha'Allah...*"

7

FLIGHT 2350

CAPTAIN ANDREW NELSON had performed the same checklist countless times over his thirty-five-year career, yet never found the sequence tedious. The responsibility of ferrying hundreds of souls safely through the air was, by itself, enough to keep him alert during each takeoff and landing. Add inclement weather, occasional mechanical difficulties, blown tires, even a couple of UFO sightings to the mix, and the risk of system failure increased.

Given all the possible variables, Nelson was proud of his perfect safety record. When his wife and children teased him, using terms like "anal" and "nerd," he welcomed their ribbing. After all, strict attention to details and perhaps a bit of luck had kept him and his passengers alive and well all these years.

"Sure I'm anal, no buts about it," he remembered answering in jest at a family gathering, drawing laughs from everyone. But over the last year, he had become increasingly short-tempered at home as he faced the inevitability of his retirement. He felt like Samson about to get a haircut and caught himself sighing...a lot. *I'm going to miss all this.*

"VR. Positive climb. V2. Flaps retracted. Gear up," announced Boynton, bringing Nelson out of his reverie.

"Trim?"

"225."

"A/P, A/T?"

Boynton clicked on the autopilot and toggled the auto trim switches upward. "Both on."

Nelson checked the LNAV and VNAV settings once again, keeping one eye on the climb profile. The plane rose steadily over Jamaica Bay. Soon it would bank slowly toward the programmed flight path. Everything seemed in order. "Autobrake? Taxi and landing lights?"

"All off, Cap. Looks like another boring day at the office."

Nelson smiled. *I'll take boring any day.*

8

A LOUD BEEP startled Rafi, snapping him out of his chant. The computer message had changed from "On the ground" to "Off the ground." In a few seconds, the target should appear. Forgetting his consternation, Rafi pointed the antenna directly ahead and turned on the booster, positioned his mouse over the ACARS icon and clicked.

After a brief pause, the word *SEARCHING...* began to blink once a second. *"Come on! Do your thing."* Seconds went by. Then... *TARGET ACQUIRED* appeared on the screen.

Rafi raised his fist. "Yes!"

"How does this program work?" Rafi had asked its creator, Firouz Ahmed, during his training.

"Remember *Star Trek*?" Ahmed replied.

"Who doesn't?"

"Think of this as a kind of tractor beam, like they had on an episode of the original TV series," Ahmed explained. "Once the target is acquired and you click ENTER, my program does two things, assuming the plane's auto-pilot system is turned on. Most pilots activate the A/P between five hundred and a thousand feet of vertical climb.

47

"First, through a boosted signal from your computer, the program fools, or "spoofs" the airplane's GPS navigation system into thinking it is on course, when it's really not. Second, the program instructs the plane to turn toward the signal's source—your computer. Ergo, the tractor-beam reference. Think of it as a hands-free joystick.

Rafi asked the obvious question. "What if the pilot cancels the autopilot and takes back manual control of the plane?"

Ahmed clapped his hands once. "Excellent question! I've created a solution, but it involves timing and divine providence. Just do your job and push ENTER. Allah will do the rest."

There it was. At least, he thought so. There were other planes taking off from different runways at the same time. Rafi could only guess that he was looking at the right one. No matter, the computer told him it had locked onto the proper ping, just as Ahmed described.

The *Magnificence* had just passed under the Verrazano Narrows Bridge and was entering Lower New York Bay. The time had come. Rafi gazed at his computer screen, which read, COMMENCE CAPTURE? Taking a deep breath, he clicked ENTER and resumed rocking in his chair. *"Insha'Allah, Insha'Allah..."*

9

ALPHA ATLANTIC FLIGHT 2350
6:23 P.M.

BOTH PILOTS felt a slight bump as if the plane had hit minor turbulence. Each checked the flight guidance panel. The settings hadn't changed but something didn't feel right. And why wasn't the plane banking as programmed?

"Cap…"

"I know," Nelson replied. Pushing the panel's A/P DISENGAGE button, his finger failed to feel the familiar click. The light stayed on. He pushed again…and again. No matter how hard he pressed, the button wouldn't budge. Both pilots tried the auto-pilot overrides on their yokes, with the same result.

As the plane continued to increase speed, it also began to descend. Feeling the first pangs of helplessness, Nelson and Boynton looked at each other and frowned. Each pilot wrestled with his control column. Both yokes failed to respond.

"Cap, what the hell…?"

Ignoring his co-pilot, Nelson spoke into his headset. "Tower, this is Triple-A 2350…"

"Roger, Triple-A 2350. You are off-course. Repeat, you are…"

"Tower, we know," interrupted Nelson. "Cannot disengage auto. Repeat, cannot disengage..."

"Triple-A 2350. Change heading immediately!"

There was no time for argument. Never in his thirty-five-year career had Captain Nelson uttered this ominous word. "Mayday. Mayday. Triple-A 2350. We have lost control. Descending rapidly."

Aware that they were mere seconds from impact, Boynton keyed his cabin mike. "Attendants, prepare passengers for a water landing. We're going down. Repeat, prepare for a water landing." Over the roar of the engines, he could hear a rising tide of screams coming from the cabin.

It was all happening so fast. Helpless, Captain Nelson tore his gaze from the A/P panel, looked out his cockpit window and gasped. "My god!"

10

NO MATTER how many times he had simulated the Plan, seeing it play out on the computer screen left Rafi in awe. Once he clicked ENTER, the message TARGET ACQUIRED quickly changed to ACARS CAPTURED, then DESTINATION ALTERED.

Two seconds later, COURSE LOCKED appeared. Firouz Ahmed's brilliant program had performed to perfection. In a few seconds, the Great Satan would be dealt a crippling blow. As an honored martyr, Rafi would enter the Kingdom of Allah to claim his seventy-two virgins.

Looking up, the young jihadist saw the airplane bearing down on the ship. Nearly orgasmic with delight, he shot out of his chair and began jumping in place, waving his arms and shouting, *"Allahu Akbar! Allahu Akbar!"* One of his two companions slid open the balcony door and peeked out from behind its curtain. Seeing her leader dancing like a madman, she asked, "Rafi, what's the matter? What's...?"

A deafening roar drowned out her scream.

Ibrahim al Rafjani welcomed the winged vessel of death into his open arms.

11

THE *MAGNIFICENCE* had entered Lower New York Bay, merging with the Atlantic Ocean. Sharon was tired of waiting. Rising from the deck chair and her husband's embrace, she returned to the suite, shed her clothes and donned one of the life vests. Sauntering back onto the deck, she leaned against the railing and beckoned with her finger. "Okay, my big hunka, hunka love. No more excuses. We're out of sight and I'm going out of my mind. Come and rescue this damsel in distress."

Duncan scrambled to his feet, hustled to the room and clicked on the door's "DO NOT DISTURB" sign. So captivated by his wife's brazen invitation, he failed to notice a whining sound, increasing in volume by the second, coming from the opposite side of the ship.

Shedding his own clothes on the way back to the balcony, he pointed to Sharon's life vest and shouted, "Orange never looked so…"

It was as if time stood still. One second, Sharon was standing all but nude against the railing with a smile on her face. The next, a tremendous jolt ejected her overboard and slammed her husband into the sliding glass balcony door, shattering it into pieces. Before he could register pain, a gigantic blast of fire consumed Duncan Richards and almost all of the ship's six-thousand occupants.

Chased by a blinding maelstrom of fire, Sharon was falling backward. Struggling against her fate was futile, yet she kicked and clawed—first imploring, then cursing a God that would rip her from life so callously. Thoughts of Duncan and the twins fueled her rage. Was this her atonement for a great marriage, good health and unexpected fortune?

Jolted breathless by an even greater impact, Sharon's backside slammed into Lower New York Bay. Breaching the surface in a few seconds, she repeatedly gasped for air. The cold water had shocked her into awareness. Temporarily paralyzed, she looked upward to witness a scene so horrible—so surreal—it would remain etched in her mind for the rest of her life.

As she passed into a merciful, dark void, poet Dylan Thomas came to mind: *Do not go gentle into that good night...*

Eventually, hands from a passing boat reached out to grasp her limp body.

12

TRIPLE-A flight 2350, traveling nearly four-hundred miles per hour with 420,000 pounds of jet fuel, plowed into the portside center of the *Magnificence of the Seas*, which carried three million gallons of heavy "Bunker C" fuel. The deafening explosion rattled all five New York City boroughs, Long Island and the eastern half of New Jersey. In the fading daylight, its mushroom cloud could be seen as far away as Providence, Hartford and Philadelphia.

Everyone inside the 777 was instantly cremated. Nearly everyone outside suffered the same fate. Cruise ship passengers "lucky" enough to survive the initial blast were either ejected into the bay or incapacitated, awaiting the fiery vortex that would kill them in mere seconds.

Within minutes of the blast, a dozen news helicopters raced toward the scene. Initial pictures confirmed everyone's worst fears. The huge cruise ship, engulfed in flames, had been severed in two by the airplane's impact. Every television and radio station in the country interrupted scheduled programming with sensational BREAKING NEWS reports and live network feeds, riveting the nation's attention on the collision's horrific aftermath.

Hospitals within a seventy-five-mile radius of the incident were put on mass casualty alert. The Sandy Hook Coast Guard fleet, accompanied by scores of pleasure boats and nearby commercial ships, raced to the scene. Coming as close to the conflagration as possible, hundreds of volunteers joined with Coast Guard personnel to pull both living and dead victims from the bay. Aeromedical helicopters whisked survivors to the nearest triage centers.

All commercial flights leaving New York City area airports were immediately grounded by the FAA "...until further notice." Fighter jets from Griffiss and McGuire Air Force bases were dispatched to circle the greater New York City area, threatening to shoot down any unauthorized aircraft that dared to enter the emergency "No Fly Zone."

Thousands of National Guard troops from Fort Hamilton and nearby military bases mustered to activate "Empire Shield," Homeland Security's plan to prevent all road traffic coming into or leaving New York City in the event of a terrorist attack.

Jockeying for a ratings advantage, television reporters spewed superlatives: "enormous; massive; spectacular; epic; colossal..." Comparisons to previous incidents were running rampant. "...potentially the largest death toll of any attack by an unknown adversary on U.S. soil; "...greater than the casualties of Pearl Harbor and 9-11 combined!"

The President of the United States was scheduled to address the nation at nine p.m. She was preempted an hour and a half earlier by a YouTube broadcast that immediately went viral and was re-broadcast on all the major TV networks.

Seven figures in black face masks and holding AK-47s stood in front of a solid white background. Their leader stepped forward to read a proclamation, his words distorted by a voice changer. "We soldiers of Allah and members of al-Qaeda in America, declare war on your decadent country. We live among you as friends, family and associates, but in truth, we are your enemies. We have many ways to kill you. Today's attacks prove once more that your airplanes are vulnerable to the wrath of Almighty Allah.

"Know that we will strike again and again in the manners, times and places of our choosing. We can and will destroy your decadent way of life. You must release all followers of Islamic jihad from your prisons. Your leaders must bow to Allah's will and sharia law. Be afraid! Be...very...afraid!"

To emphasize their leader's words, the remaining six masked terrorists stepped forward, raised their weapons overhead and shouted in unison, *"Allahu Akbar!"* The video ended with the black flag of jihad waving, surrounded by a field of computer-generated flames.

13

THE WHITE HOUSE
WEST WING
7:45 P.M.

PRESIDENT ELIZABETH STANTON stood at the head of a large conference table, barely able to control her anger. Large television screens dedicated to all the major networks surrounded the Situation Room. The networks were playing and re-playing the terrorist video, interspersed with eyewitness accounts of the attack and footage of the charred remains of the partially submerged cruise ship. While the rest of the screens were muted, sound from the one behind the president was on. The normally staid NBC News anchor Brian Williams was gesturing wildly toward his monitor. "How could something like this happen again...in New York, for god's sake?"

Stanton had seen enough. Her blood boiling, she muted the TV, slammed her hand down on the long conference table and screamed at her national security team. "Who the hell are these people? Who dropped the ball and let this happen. Somebody talk to me!"

Like school children vying for their teacher's attention, everyone stood and began shouting. After a few seconds of heated cacophony, Stanton shook her head in disgust.

Raising both hands for quiet, she pointed to the Secretary of Homeland Security, Margaret Smith. "Margo, tell me something I don't know."

"Madam President," Smith began, looking around the room for support, "I regret to inform you this incident took us all by surprise. What we know is that a Boeing 777 took off from JFK and abruptly nose-dived into the world's largest cruise ship in Lower New York Bay. Less than two minutes went by from takeoff to collision. It happened so fast, there was no time to intercept or divert the airplane. From this video, we must assume that this was a planned terrorist attack..."

"We must make no such assumption until the facts are in," interrupted National Security Advisor Jack Gardner. Waving his hand toward the television for emphasis, he added, "This video could be nothing more than a radical group seeking attention. The airplane could have malfunctioned..."

"Please!" broke in General Mike Jablonsky, the Chairman of the Joint Chiefs of Staff. "For years, we've been warning that something like this would happen. What did we get from the last two administrations? Politically correct bullshit, that's what!" The sixty-year-old fireplug's face was turning red with frustration. In a mocking tone, he sneered, "Don't offend the Muslim community. We might hurt their feelings. Profiling is un-American. The vast majority of Muslims are good citizens who want to live in peace. Al-Qaeda is on the run. Blah, blah, blah..."

It was the chairman's turn to point at the largest television, gesturing for the president to raise the volume once more. A multi-split screen showed hooded men and women in burqas dancing in the streets of major American and foreign cities.

Many were burning American flags and holding signs with slogans like *Death to America; Die, Zionist Pigs; Allah is Great!*

"Well, ladies and gentlemen," Jablonsky followed, "to quote a radical black preacher, 'The chickens have come home to roost!'"

Everyone in the room stood, gesturing and shouting. In an effort to quell the chaos, President Stanton held her hands high and screamed, "Quiet! Sit down. Everyone. Now!"

After a few seconds of rancorous stares, everyone sat and focused their attention on the feisty president. Tall and attractive, with green eyes that could burn a hole through steel, fifty-two- year-old Elizabeth Stanton had been a highly successful governor of South Carolina. Absent the shrill voice that so often derailed other female pretenders to the office, the feisty "Blue Dog" Democrat spoke in a commanding tone that drew attention to her concise, confident arguments. In her successful campaign for the presidency, Stanton had captivated the media with her quick wit, while eviscerating all opponents with a combination of daggered logic, a stubborn countenance and creative condescension. Margaret Thatcher of the United Kingdom had earned the moniker "Iron Lady." Early in her political career, the media dubbed Stanton the "Steel Magnolia," which added glamor to her reputation for competency and a no-nonsense style of leadership.

The governor's marketing slogan "Stand with Stanton" and song *"Lean on Me"*—the 1972 Bill Withers hit—added "grass root" support to her e-mail, social media and ground offensives.

Stanton's stump speech was simple and devastating. "Men, you've had more than your share of chances to screw things up. Over the last hundred years, you've managed through greed, vanity and downright stupidity, to lead our country to the brink of disaster. Now get the hell out of the way. Let this woman clean house and pick up your dirty laundry!"

It was a message that resonated with over eighty percent of women voters, who came out in record numbers to rocket Elizabeth Stanton to a landslide victory over her hapless opponent. Her hawkish attitude garnered half the male vote as well.

Stanton knew she was inheriting a nightmare of colossal failures. The United States was over twenty trillion dollars in debt. After years of feckless appeasement, America no longer commanded respect as the world's mightiest superpower. Despite its own growing pains and corruption, China had overtaken the U.S. as the largest economy and was lobbying the United Nations for the yuan to replace the dollar as the world's primary reserve currency.

With the help of a conservative majority in both houses of Congress, Stanton had begun fulfilling her most urgent domestic campaign pledges: tax breaks for small business, eliminating thousands of onerous and unnecessary regulations, and reopening previously closed domestic oil and gas leases. Defying threats of retaliation and lawsuits by federal employee unions, the president had used "executive privilege" to furlough thousands of unnecessary and corrupt government workers—her pledge to "clean house." Two months into her first term of office, over eighty percent of Americans "stood with Stanton."

Unleashing the nation's stifled economy had already begun to show signs of success. Deficits were shrinking and businesses were hiring hundreds of thousands of full-time employees. Many who had given up looking for work were once again pursuing new careers.

The president's harsh rhetoric, strict sanctions and punishing import quotas on nations that were taking advantage of America's largess, had yielded few concessions from self-serving competitor nations. Like jackals circling a kill, America's enemies were eager to pounce on any sign of weakness from this female president.

Waiting for everyone in the Situation Room to cease talking, Elizabeth Stanton gestured for calm. "Arguing among ourselves will do no good. I need reliable information. If those hooded vermin are responsible for today's attacks, we need to find out who they are and stop them before any more of these atrocities occur."

Pointing to Jablonsky, she ordered, "General, don't talk. Just listen. Effective immediately, I want all our armed forces around the world put on maximum alert. Mobilize the National Guard in all fifty states to assist local police and corral any violence that results from this incident."

Shifting her gaze to the Secretary of Homeland Security, she added, "Margo, I want you to contact the FAA. Ground all the nation's outgoing flights until further notice. Use military fighter jets as needed to escort incoming flights to their destinations. Make it clear to all incoming crews that any deviation in their landing patterns will be deemed a hostile act and dealt with accordingly."

"You mean shot down?" Secretary Smith asked.

"Only if necessary," Stanton answered. "Also…"

A collective gasp halted the president in mid-sentence. Everyone was pointing to the muted televisions around the room. Stanton looked up to see smoke pouring out of two familiar buildings. Sound wasn't necessary. Above the FOX NEWS screen's yellow and red BREAKING NEWS alert, the captions read, "SAN FRANCISCO—TRANSAMERICA BUILDING HIT BY PLANE;" and "AIRPLANE HITS CHICAGO LANDMARK."

Covered in a blanket of doom, the Situation Room was oddly silent. Each of its occupants stared at the televisions, paralyzed at the visions before them. Margo Smith broke the spell with three ominous words. "We're too late."

The president sat in her chair, gesturing for the rest to follow her lead. In a level voice laced with rage, she addressed her press secretary. "Jackie, put the speech writers in overdrive. Move my address to the nation back one hour to ten p.m. The rest of you," she scanned the room, looking at each member of her national security team eye-to-eye, "do what is necessary to prepare for the worst. Americans won't stand for these attacks. We have to expect riots, mosque burnings and murders." Slamming her hand again on the conference table, she ended with, "By God, I'm not going to stand by and let a few maniacs destroy the country on my watch!"

With that, President Elizabeth Stanton exited the room. No one dared confront the leader of the free world as she retired to the family quarters. Breaking down in tears, she received a bear hug from Edward, her campaign manager and husband of twenty-six years, along with a double shot of whiskey.

"Thousands died today...on my watch," she cried. "What can I do? How am I..."

"Liz, you're the strongest person I know," Ed interrupted with an iron jaw of certainty. "You have the power to stop this. You'll know what to do. The critics can go to hell."

14

THE WHITE HOUSE
OVAL OFFICE
10 P.M.

PRESIDENT ELIZABETH STANTON stared into the camera with a look of steely determination. "My fellow Americans, once again terrorists have attacked our nation. In each of three coordinated acts, a commercial airliner was hijacked and deliberately flown into highly populated and iconic targets— a cruise ship in New York's Lower Bay, the Transamerica Building in San Francisco and the Willis Tower—also known as the Sears Tower—in Chicago. All three have been destroyed. The number of casualties won't be available for days, but it looks like the total will be one of the greatest single-day losses of life in American history.

"Immediately after the first attack on the *Magnificence of the Seas* and after each subsequent event, I ordered Federal Emergency Response teams into action. As I speak to you tonight, thousands of military reserves, aided by state and local law enforcement, fire departments and medical teams, are hard at work bringing survivors to safety and accounting for casualties. I assure you that their work will continue non-stop until the last victim is located."

Stanton paused and looked past the camera. "Greg, please turn off the teleprompter." Muffled protests could be heard from the communications director and the television crew. "I mean it. Turn the damn thing off! The American people know what happened. They deserve better than a load of statistics."

After a few seconds, the president looked back into the camera. "Unlike President Bush after 9-11, I refuse to engage in lofty rhetoric about our country's strength and determination to stamp out terrorism. Talk is cheap. You are beyond angry, and so am I.

"You want to know why, with all the elaborate safeguards in place to prevent aerial attacks, three airplanes could be hijacked and once again flown into vulnerable targets. You want to know what we're going to do about cowards who hide behind ski masks, spouting hatred and threats toward our country and way of life.

"From the communication between pilots and towers, here's what we know. In each instance, after takeoff, the airplane's autopilot could not be disengaged. Somehow, someone gained control of the guidance system of each plane and directed it toward its target. Our best technical minds will soon discover the methods used and what countermeasures we can implement to prevent similar attacks in the future. Moreover, I will not sleep until we find out who planned these atrocities and bring them to justice.

"Americans, you know that these attacks were not carried out by Swedish grandmothers. Yet, officially we refuse to use the terms 'Islamic terrorists' and 'radical Islam' for fear of offending the Muslim community. We must face the truth. Political correctness has hijacked common sense.

"It's high time we take the gloves off and stop handicapping our efforts to fight terrorism. Over the last few years, our foreign policy has been one of apologies, appeasement and avoiding confrontation with our adversaries. At home and abroad, allies and enemies perceive America to be weak and insincere. "Red lines" mean nothing if they are not backed up by serious consequences. The bottom line? Today's incidents are the result of a decade of misguided leadership.

"This mindset has to stop. Actions must replace rhetoric. Therefore, I have issued the following orders be put into effect immediately.

"First, the Federal Aviation Administration will ground all private and commercial aircraft until we have installed effective deterrents to the type of incidents we saw today. As opposed to the hijackings of 9-11, perpetrated by passengers armed with box-cutters, aviation analysts are convinced that today's attacks were unmanned and technical in nature. If this is true, countermeasures already exist. Once the specific causes of today's hijackings are confirmed, we will retrofit every commercial airliner with the appropriate defensive technology. If even one life can be saved in the future, cost will not be a factor.

"Second, I am instructing the Transportation Safety Administration, the TSA, to disseminate a list of new procedures to all employees. From now on, airport screeners will be using the Israeli protocol of profiling. To those who condemn this, I ask you a question. When is the last time someone hijacked an Israeli airplane? The answer is 1968, almost fifty years ago, and it's the only time. Profiling? Hell yes, we're going to use it...because it works."

President Stanton paused for effect. "After 9-11 and yesterday's incidents, you have witnessed Muslims dancing in the streets, burning our flag and shouting slogans like 'Death to America.' Already I'm hearing reports of armed militias burning American mosques and assaulting persons of the Islamic faith. We will not tolerate such retaliatory measures. Anyone found harming persons or property, no matter what their religious faith, will be prosecuted to the fullest extent of the law.

"Finally, let me get personal and address the law-abiding citizens of Muslim communities. Home-grown terrorists live among you. You know who they are, but because of fear and intimidation, you remain silent. Yet you demand respect and protection from your fellow countrymen who are outraged by your passive complicity. You call us infidels. Many of you rejoice when we are killed and injured in spectacular attacks like the three events of today.

"To those who enjoy the liberty and lifestyle that American citizenship provides, you must make a choice of allegiance between your country and radical Islam. I call on every Muslim citizen to reveal the names of these terrorists to the proper authorities. You can do so anonymously without fear of retaliation.

"You cannot have it both ways. Know that we are watching and listening to you and everyone around you. The days of political correctness are over. Be assured that we are not at war with your religion, only the radical hijackers of your faith.

America is in survival mode, and I will not tolerate any actions against our country, its citizens or the freedoms we enjoy. Any of you found aiding and abetting terrorists will be arrested and prosecuted with the same vigor as your radical brethren. 'Freedom of speech' in the First Amendment to our Constitution does not include insurrection or inciting violence against America or its citizenry. Therefore, anyone who preaches violence or plans violent acts against this country will be apprehended and prosecuted as well."

"To those in other countries who try to take advantage of today's events by launching attacks against us or our allies, be advised that our military is ready and capable of striking anywhere in the world. Do not assume that the events of today are a sign of American weakness or lack of resolve.

Fire seemed to shoot from her eyes as she spoke the next words. "And to the leaders of Iran in particular, know this. If you dare to launch one nuclear-armed missile toward the state of Israel, I will consider it an act of war against our country as well. We will join our ally in making sure your country will cease to exist. This president is angry as hell and my hand is on the trigger!"

A collective gasp could be heard from everyone in the Oval Office, as well as every newsroom in the country. *Has the President of the United States lost her mind?*

After another pause—this time at least five seconds—Stanton resumed her address in a measured tone. "Finally, let me speak to the families of those who have fallen this day. On behalf of the entire country, I offer you my heartfelt condolences. I will salute your loved ones, heroes all, as soon as possible, in a formal ceremony. To the injured, families of victims, emergency personnel and volunteers, know that support from your government will follow, as in the aftermath of 9-11.

"Nothing I say this evening could possibly be adequate. Nothing I do will bring your loved ones back. I can only make these promises to you and every citizen of the greatest country on Earth. As God is my witness, I will do whatever is necessary to defeat the scourge of terrorism on our soil, and I will do whatever it takes to preserve our way of life." She paused once more, obviously fighting back tears of anger.

"May God bless all of you in this time of tribulation, and may God continue to bless the United States of America."

As the picture faded to network coverage, President Elizabeth Stanton rose from behind the Resolute Desk and walked slowly out of the Oval Office. She seemed lost in a trance. No one dared voice a comment. No one, that is, except Mike Jablonsky, the Chairman of the Joint Chiefs of Staff. "That was either a foolish attempt at political suicide," he growled to his adjutant, "or the gutsiest goddamned speech I've ever heard."

DAY TWO

15

DR. ABU MAZRA was beside himself with joy. He and his assistant, Firouz Ahmed, had anticipated failure in at least one of the three attacks, but all of them had worked to perfection.

Watching the dancing and cries of ecstasy within his mosque, Imam Mustafa Shabbah sported a rare smile and held out his arms to embrace the mastermind who had created this audacious, multi-faceted plan.

"The Great Satan is weeping tears of blood," he shouted over the celebration. "Glory to Allah! He has blessed us this day with three victories. Thousands of infidels are dead and gravely wounded. Muhammad, my son, your video was an additional stroke of genius. America is quaking in fear.

"We must not lose sight of our ultimate goal. The Great Satan is wounded, but not yet defeated. Now is the time to strike another set of blows, while the enemy is distracted." Once again he rested a hand on Abu Mazra's shoulder. "You, my son, have the honor of preparing our warriors for the next phase."

Ever cautious, the professor asked, "Imam, did you see the president's address last evening?"

"*Pah!*" Shabbah spat. "The president is a woman. All women are weak. She has the mouth of a lion but the claws of a chicken. We will watch her weep helplessly as this country descends into chaos."

Shabbah gripped Abu Mazra's shoulders and drew within inches of the professor's face. With teeth stained by years of chewing tobacco and breath that stank of garlic, Imam Mustafa Shabbah shouted with the passion of a crazed zealot, "Notify the soldiers of Allah. Commence Phase Two."

16

CAPITAL HEALTH MEDICAL CENTER
PENNINGTON, NEW JERSEY

"HEY, CHAMP. Welcome back."

At first, she could only hear the voice. Within seconds, her eyes adjusted to see a young man in green hospital scrubs. His badge read WILLIAMS. Two nurses flanked him. All three were staring at her like she was some kind of lab animal. Feeling groggy, Sharon Richards could tell she was tethered to a bed. When she tried to move her head, needle-like pain coursed down the length of her spine.

Gasping, she mouthed, "Water." One of the nurses put a straw to Sharon's lips. Fighting through the pain, she sucked in a mouthful and forced herself to swallow.

"You're one very lucky lady," the man said. "There were few survivors. Almost everyone aboard your cruise ship was killed. Can you speak?"

"What? Where am I?" she croaked.

"You're in a New Jersey hospital, hon," said one of the nurses. You've been unconscious for more than twelve hours since the..." she paused, searching for the right word, "...incident. Do you remember your name?"

It took a few seconds for her to form the words. "Richards…Sharon…Richards." Tears welled in her eyes as the weight of the young man's ominous words hit home.

One of the nurses left the room, no doubt to deliver Sharon's name to her superiors.

Sharon added, "M…my husband…twins?"

"I'm sorry," Williams answered, soberly shaking his head. "It's doubtful any of them survived." He held up an orange life jacket. "This is what you were wearing…nothing else, when the Coast Guard found you," he added, turning slightly red in the face. "When they brought you in, you were unconscious but violent. For your own good, we had to restrain you. I'm sorry…"

Another man entered the room. He was dressed in a suit coat and tie. "Mrs. Richards, is it?" he asked in a clipped, matter-of-fact voice. Not waiting for an answer, he continued, "I'm Dr. Panjamaddi. Everyone calls me Dr. P."

Saying nothing in response, Sharon blinked back a tear. "You've had a nasty fall," the doctor added. "What deck of the ship were you on?"

"Fourteen. Why?"

Dr. Williams shook his head. "X-rays show you've suffered no broken bones or fractures. That's amazing, considering you must have fallen a couple hundred feet into the bay. Your life vest must have cushioned the impact. Apparently, all you received was a world class chiropractic adjustment. You'll be sore for a few…"

"What happened?" she interrupted.

"Yes, of course, you wouldn't know, would you?" The doctor pointed to a small television hanging from the ceiling across the room. "You've been unconscious for half a day, Mrs. Richards. Once you answer a few questions, we'll turn on the TV and you can catch up on the news." He nodded to one of the female nurses holding a clipboard and pen. "Now, what is your date of birth...?"

Drugged with painkillers, exhausted and overcome with grief, Sharon steeled herself to answer five minutes of the doctor's questions. Before leaving her room, one of the team members released her tethers and turned on the television. "This will come as another shock to you, hon," she said. "Believe me, you're not alone. Yesterday was a nightmare for everyone. Try to remain calm, lay flat on your back and get some rest, okay? The doctor says later today you can be released, with some painkillers, of course."

Sharon Richards watched in horror as one of the most daunting days in American history played out on the screen. Stock markets worldwide were in freefall, each index reaching its trading curb within minutes of opening. With all U.S. airlines grounded indefinitely, the American economy had basically come to a halt. Excepting essential government personnel, most workers were on involuntary vacation.

Following President Stanton's address, millions had taken to the streets, demanding retribution. Defying the president's order for restraint, many mosques throughout the country had been torched. Anyone in Muslim garb who dared celebrate these attacks was assaulted or killed. "It is becoming evident," one TV commentator posited, "that authorities throughout America are losing control of the populace. Anarchy is becoming the norm."

Taking in the details of the attacks, Sharon reverted to the FBI analyst she had been for the last quarter century. Most domestic threats come from harmless amateurs—all talk and no action. These carefully coordinated assaults were planned and executed by a creative, organized and determined insurgent cell. She played back the masked terrorist's rant three times. One sentence stood out over the others. *"Know that we will strike again and again in the manners, times and places of our choosing."*

More than the tragic news reports, more than the hysterical conjecture by media pundits, this threat sent a chill up Sharon's injured spine, causing her to flinch in pain once again.

They've only begun.

17

HAVERTOWN, PENNSYLVANIA
4 P.M.

SHARON RICHARDS slowly exited the limousine that had driven her home from the New Jersey hospital. The physical pain she still suffered was augmented by inane questions fired at her from a small gaggle of reporters.

"Any news of Duncan and your children?"

"Mrs. Richards, how do you feel about losing your family to terrorists?"

"How did you manage to fall off the ship without any injuries?"

She held up both hands, gesturing for them to stop. "I've just lost my family. I have no comment at this time. Please...leave me alone!"

Disregarding her pain, Sharon marched toward her front door, where two familiar faces waited to greet her. One was her next door neighbor, Phyllis Schumacher, who had been glued to the television for news of her famous friend. She had Sharon's spare key. The other was Gloria Hyde, an attorney with Summerfield, Patton, Bromfield and Hyde, trustees of Duncan's inherited fortune. Gloria had brought a large bouquet of flowers—a burst of gaiety in sharp contrast to the somber occasion.

With the press on her heels, Sharon gestured for both women to follow her into the house, where they embraced. "I'm so sorry, hon," blubbered Phyllis. "Your boys…" Her voice gave way to wordless weeping.

Gloria was slightly more reserved since she knew the family only on a professional basis. "I just want you to know that all of us at the firm are on call if you need anything. And here…" She passed Sharon a letter. "Please read this whenever. No hurry. Everything's under control…"

"I'm not ready to talk about the money, Gloria, but thanks for coming by. I'll be in touch soon."

Gloria closed the door behind her and Phyllis held out her arms for another hug. "Hon, if there's anything…"

Sharon tried to comfort her neighbor and friend, patting her back in the embrace. "I know, Phyllis, I know. If you can understand, I just want to be alone for a while, okay? You'll be the first I'll call if I need anything, I promise."

Crying, the neighbor collected herself, nodded and left.

Sharon peeked through the front window and scanned the yard. The reporters were departing, no doubt miffed that they hadn't elicited any further comments from their prey.

She walked back into the living room and collapsed in Duncan's favorite lounge chair, knowing that it would be the closest thing to his embrace. Minutes went by. Was it the painkillers or was the old grandfather clock ticking a metronomic dirge, as if to say, *all you have now is time?*

Sharon closed her eyes and remembered her last minute on the balcony with Duncan. "Come and rescue this damsel in distress," she had said, provocatively clothed only in her life vest.

What had he replied? "Orange never looked so..."

Then the jolt and it was over—her husband, lover, childhood friend—gone in a blast of hellfire, and she was falling backward—down, down, down—until a bone-chilling blow knocked her unconscious. She counted out six ticks of the clock, guessing that was about how long it would have taken to fall off the ship and hit the water. Six seconds...and her life had changed forever.

And her boys, Dougie and Damon. Where were they when it happened? What were their last thoughts? Only fourteen, the twins were too young to show promising futures, but the signs were there. Both were good students in school, respectful of authority and accepted by their classmates.

Dougie, a type-A personality, was outgoing—a clown and risk-taker, looking for laughs and defying gravity. He had the scars and broken bones to prove it.

Damon was type-B—quiet and reserved, serious and cautious. The only scar was on his left hand. He had cut it peeling back the lid on a can of Vienna sausage.

She opened her eyes. *But what does all that matter now? Duncan, Dougie and Damon. For the rest of my life, they'll be only memories.*

"My Donut," she wailed out loud. "My pain-in-the-ass...Donut."

After staring at nothing for a half-hour, Sharon remembered the envelope Gloria Hyde had left behind. It was on the small table beside Duncan's lounge chair. Opening it, she pulled out a single page of stationery with the law firm's letterhead.

Dear Mrs. Richards,

On behalf of everyone at Summerfield, Patton, Bromfield and Hyde, we want to offer our most sincere condolences in your time of grief. No words can possibly suffice to alleviate the suffering you must be going through at this time.

Although the thought of finances must be the last thing on your mind, this letter is to assure you that, as a result of the terrorist attacks, our firm has made timely allocation adjustments to Duncan's trust appropriate to the economic downturn.

Please know that everything in the trust is secure without any loss of principal. On the contrary, our adjustments have yielded a sizable profit. When we receive a certified copy of his death certificate, all assets in Duncan's trust will revert to you as his spouse.

Meanwhile, we have taken the liberty of transferring $500,000 from the trust cash account to your checking account. If you object to this transfer or the amount, please let us know and we will make the appropriate changes.

Mrs. Richards, if there is anything we can do for you, including assisting in funeral

*arrangements, please contact Gloria Hyde.
No matter how big or small your request,
everyone at Summerfield, Patton, Bromfield
and Hyde remains ready to help.*

Sincerely, Ralph R. Patton, Attorney at Law

Sharon put the letter on the table. *You're right, Mr. Patton.
Money is the last thing on my mind, but I appreciate your
thoughtfulness.*

Girding herself for one more task, she picked up the house
phone and dialed the number of the best friend she had left
in the world, praying that he was still in his office.

FBI Special Agent-in-Charge Will Lambert picked up his
desk phone and smiled. "Well, if it isn't my favorite retired
agent. How are you, Sharon, and how's the family?"

The voice on the other end was cold as ice. "Will, my family
is dead." *Apparently he hasn't seen the local news yet.*

The words hit Lambert like a sledgehammer. The Sharon he
knew never joked about anything serious. "Talk to me."

"We were on the *Magnificence* when the plane hit,"
Sharon answered. "I was thrown overboard. Duncan and the
boys were not. They had no chance." She paused to gather
herself. "I've lost everything, Will. My family..." she choked
back a sob, "...was my life. You know that."

At fifty-six, Will Lambert was nearing his thirty-year
retirement. Six-foot-three and lean from a daily ritual of
short but extreme workouts, Lambert's countenance and

deliberate mannerisms resembled those of the mid-twentieth century actor Gary Cooper. His deep, authoritarian voice could intimidate or calm, depending on the situation. Twice divorced, he admired his attractive former second-in-command on more than the professional level but had always kept his feelings to himself.

"My god, Sharon. I don't know what to…"

"Don't say anything, Will. I'm fine, physically at least. I was wearing a life vest. It cushioned my fall from the ship. Apparently there are no broken bones. The hospital released me earlier today and I'm home now." She paused to change subjects. "I'm calling to ask a favor."

"Anything, Sharon, anything," Will answered, still rattled by her news.

"I want back in, Will. You know I was one of your best analysts. Start me at the bottom or give me back my old job as your assistant. I don't care."

Shocked again, Lambert pondered her request. He had heard about Duncan's trust. It must have been large enough to allow Sharon to retire early. *So why does she want to return to her old civil service job here in Philadelphia?* Upon reflection, the answer was obvious.

"I'm serious, Will," she continued. "One way or another, I'm going to nail the bastards who killed my family."

"Come to the office. We'll talk."

"Nine tomorrow?"

"Nine it is," Lambert answered. "And Sharon…"

"Yes?"

"…when I said anything, I meant anything."

As the line went dead, Will Lambert chastised himself. *She's lost her family and all I can think of is seeing her again. God, how I've missed that woman.*

DAY THREE

18

**SUPER 8 MOTEL
LAS VEGAS, NEVADA
THURSDAY**

MEHRALA AL-HAQ was sleeping when his iPhone buzzed. The motel clock next to his bed read 1:17 a.m. Like the other teams in Minnesota and Miami, Mehrala and his partner, Ashami Najar were battle-hardened insurgents from Syria. They had entered the U.S. with European passports. Following instructions from their coordinator in New York, both had been holed up in the Vegas motel for three days, waiting for the call. The gruff, authoritative voice on the other end was unmistakable. "Prepare Phase Two. You will be notified when to proceed."

"Is it time?" asked Ashami, sitting up in the next bed and rubbing his eyes.

Mehrala nodded, putting down his cell phone. "Get dressed. We have a lot of work to do."

They drove to a nearby storage unit. Using a rented forklift, they transferred four tons of diesel fuel in twelve fifty-five-gallon drums, ten bags of ammonium nitrate fertilizer, chemicals and ignition supplies, onto a white GMC-W4500 that had been retrofitted in advance to balance the heavy load. That they were being filmed by storage monitors was of no consequence. It was the middle of a hot Las Vegas night. No one else was around to report unusual activity, and the chances were slim to none that someone would review the tape before the bomb was detonated.

Next, Al-Haq and Najar drove to a remote location in the desert. With illumination from the moon and battery-powered lights, they prepared and electrically connected in tandem all the drums to the detonator, using the procedure that they and the other two teams had practiced many times—one that Timothy McVeigh, Michael Fortier and Terry Nichols had followed for the 1995 Oklahoma City bombing.

As the sun began its climb toward another scorching day, both men checked and re-checked their preparations. Satisfied, they closed the truck's rear door and drove back to their motel. Mehrala took the first shift, watching the truck as Ashami slept soundly in their air-conditioned room. Basking in the knowledge that soon he would be welcomed as a martyr by Allah, his lord and master, al-Haq smiled.

19

FBI REGIONAL FIELD OFFICE
PHILADELPHIA, PENNSYLVANIA
FRIDAY, 9 A.M.

AFTER FIFTEEN MINUTES of hugging and condolences from agents and staff, Sharon Richards entered the office of her former boss, Will Lambert. They embraced for more than fifteen seconds. Words were unnecessary.

Will noticed that Sharon had changed in the last two months since she had retired. With the trauma she had endured, it was understandable, but instead of shedding tears, the hard-charging, eager-to-please woman he had known now seemed stoic and distant.

"How are you holding up?" he asked, not knowing what else to say. "Have they found any...?"

"No, and they probably won't," she replied, shaking her head. "At least, they couldn't have suffered, it happened so fast."

"God, Sharon, I don't know what to say."

"No need, Will," she replied with a wan smile. "You're my only real friend now, someone I...can depend on."

"Have you made any arrangements?" he asked, bolder now. "Duncan was a hero. He was mentioned on the local news last night. And so were you. The press must have found your names on the ship's manifest. Apparently, you're the only survivor who suffered no serious injuries."

Sharon nodded, ignoring the last two remarks. *So that's why those reporters were waiting for me in front of the building.* "I had to run a press gauntlet to come up here. As to your question, I can't make any arrangements until my husband and boys are officially declared dead, so there's no hurry. Besides, the terrorist on the video made it clear that more incidents are imminent. Finding and stopping them before they strike again has to take precedent."

Lambert nodded. "When you gave notice two months ago, I said if you ever wanted to return, you could—as long as I'm the agent-in-charge, of course. But, you know I have to ask this question. In light of your tragedy, can you resume your role dispassionately and professionally, following the mandated guidelines?"

"Off the record?" she asked.

Will nodded again.

"Of course, this is personal. I wouldn't be human if it wasn't. Dispassionately? Hell no! Professionally, yes. I wasn't an agent for twenty-five years without having federal guidelines drilled into me every day. So yes, I can and will fulfill my duties as before, just with more determination to catch the bastards that are out to destroy our country. Now, how about swearing me in?"

Lambert grinned. "I'd hate to be on your shit list, lady."

For the first time, Sharon returned his smile. "Maybe the pendulum of political correctness is swinging back to our side. From what I've seen on TV, we finally have a president

94

with a backbone and the balls to match. I'd hate to be on her shit list, too."

"Which brings me to a twenty-minute phone call I received right before you came in." Lambert paused, relishing Sharon's puzzled look. "It was from someone who'd like to meet you, someone with a much higher pay grade than mine. Elizabeth Stanton."

Sharon's jaw dropped. The RAIC continued. "I told her you might find time in your busy schedule to grace her with your presence."

"You didn't," Sharon challenged.

Will chuckled. "Not exactly in those words. You have an appointment tomorrow morning at the White House. Ten a.m. sharp. The president asked to meet with you before I swear you in." He buzzed his assistant. "Shirley, please send in Agent Hampton."

A tall, thin African-American man, nattily dressed in a three-piece suit, entered and closed the door. Agent Ron Hampton held out his arms to Sharon. Tears were in his eyes. "I'm so...sorry. Gonna miss...Papa Dough," he blubbered, using his nickname for Duncan. Together, Ron and Duncan had devised a plan to apprehend two of the nation's most notorious criminals. Along the way, they had forged a strong friendship.

Sharon hugged him. "We're going to catch the scumbags who did this, aren't we, Hamp?"

Ron released her and stood back, admiring her resolve. "Damn right!"

DAY FOUR

20

THE WHITE HOUSE
WEST WING
FRIDAY, 10 A.M.

SHARON RICHARDS pretended to read the latest edition of *U.S. News & World Report*. Her hands shook and her head throbbed from the lingering aftereffects of her two-hundred-foot fall off the doomed cruise ship.

Madelyn Forsyth, the president's personal secretary, noticed her nervousness. "Is this your first time in the White House, Mrs. Richards?"

"No, I was here with my sixth-grade class," Sharon replied. "This is my first time to meet the president, though. Do you have a couple of aspirin?" she added. "My head is killing me."

Forsyth pulled out a bottle of Bayer aspirin from her desk drawer, handed it to Sharon with a smile and pointed to a nearby water cooler. Madelyn was used to putting people at ease. "The president may seem a little gruff on TV. God knows she has good reason with all that's happened recently. But I assure you, she's quite pleasant in person. I think you'll like her."

"It's just...I have no idea why I'm here," Sharon stated after downing two of the pills.

Forsyth smiled again and answered, "Sorry, my lips are sealed. But I can tell you that you're not being taken to the woodshed."

Forsyth's console buzzed, followed by the familiar voice of President Stanton. "Madelyn, please send in Mrs. Richards."

The secretary rose from her seat and opened the ornately decorated door. Gesturing for Sharon to follow, she announced officially, "The president will see you now."

Sharon took a deep breath and walked into the Oval Office. Two of the most famous women in America sat across from each other in front of the famous Resolute Desk. Both rose in unison to greet her.

President Elizabeth Stanton smiled warmly and held out her hand. "So you're the woman who survived a fall from a cruise ship...without a scratch." Her demeanor instantly changed from light to serious. "It's a pleasure to meet you, Mrs. Richards. Please accept my most sincere condolences for the loss of your loved ones."

Sharon's mouth was dry but she managed to answer, "Thank you, Madam President."

The other woman approached Sharon and held out her hand as well. "Do you know who I am?"

"Of course, I do. You're one of my heroes, Ms. Mills," Sharon replied, shaking the woman's hand.

Lena Mills was a legend. Suffering an abusive childhood, the former nightclub stripper had used determination, revenge and, some claimed, mystical powers to become one of America's most outspoken media superstars. So potent was her popular message, she carried her version of "Shock and Awe" to the halls of Congress and forced a sitting president to confront a devastating secret from his past, bringing the nation to the brink of polarized anarchy.

Tall, blonde and physically fit, Mills was in her mid-sixties but didn't look a day older than forty. When asked her age, she usually deflected her answer by quoting a former vice-president. "You know, sixty is the new fifty-nine," Al Gore had quipped with a straight face during a television interview. "It's the only funny thing the fat hypocrite ever said," Lena commented.

Seeing the puzzled look on Sharon's face, the president gestured for everyone to sit. "Sharon—may I call you by your first name?"

Richards nodded. "Of, course, Madam President."

The president smiled. "Then please return the favor by calling me Liz, at least while we're not in front of an audience, okay?"

Sharon felt awkward and hesitated, but in a couple of seconds, nodded again. "I'll try. How did you know I used to work with the FBI?"

"One of my staff heard a news report about you. We've studied your twenty-five-year career with the FBI. Your analysis of terror cells and record of thwarting domestic attacks is exemplary.

"Let me get right to the point. Have you kept up with your FBI training?"

Lena broke in. "Liz means can you still kick ass?"

Stanton smiled. "Spoken like the shy, demure Lena we all know and love." The president looked at Sharon and waited for an answer.

"I can hold my own," Sharon answered. "I don't understand…"

Stanton sat forward, eager to continue. "I had a lengthy conversation yesterday with your former FBI resident agent-in-charge, Will Lambert."

Sharon nodded. "Yes, he told me."

"Did he tell you what we discussed?"

"Only that you asked to meet with me. Other than that, I'm in the dark…"

"Our discussion was about you—all about you," Stanton interrupted. "After talking with him, I'm convinced that you're uniquely qualified for a crucial assignment I'm about to describe. What I'm about to reveal only a handful of people will know, and I want to keep it that way. Understand?"

Letting her words hang in the air, the president added, "Sharon, do you swear to keep everything we discuss in this room today in strict confidence?"

Sharon stared into Stanton's eyes, then Lena's. *They're going to drop a big one on me.* "I do."

Satisfied, the president continued. "Our country is at a crossroads. You've seen the news. You, more than anyone else, know what it means to be the victim of a terrorist attack."

The president paused. "Let me be frank. I've been in office for two months and already I'm mired in the consequences of bad foreign and domestic policy left behind by my predecessor. My primary mandate as president is the safety of all American citizens. With these attacks, I've failed to deliver on this most important priority. We must find the terrorists behind these assaults and neutralize them before they attack again, but because of legal restraints, federal law enforcement agencies are prohibited from arresting U.S. citizens without ironclad evidence of their involvement in terror activity. In other words, we have to catch the bastards in the act before we can do anything about it, and even if we have the proof, we must treat the attacks as crimes, not acts of war, and subject to the justice system's rules of procedure."

"I'm aware of these restrictions," Sharon replied. "I worked around them in the FBI whenever possible. A lot of good arrests are thrown out because of procedural technicalities. We call them 'rules of disengagement.' It's one of the reasons I retired."

"But now you want to come back," Lena broke in.

Sharon glared at her with defiance. "Yes. My family was killed by these people and I want revenge. There, I said it. Does that disqualify my return to duty?"

President Stanton looked at Lena. Both smiled. "On the contrary," Stanton continued, "it makes you ideal for our mission. I need someone like you, a former FBI terror analyst, who is not a current employee of any government agency, to positively identify the leaders of this homegrown jihadist organization. Then we will remove these bastards to a remote location where they'll be interrogated, using any means necessary to find the rest of the bad actors and foil their plans for future terrorist attacks."

Sharon's eyebrows raised in surprise. "*Any* means necessary?"

"You heard me right," Stanton replied, with a look of determination. "I promised the American people that I would do whatever is necessary to bring these terrorists to justice. I didn't specify what kind of justice."

Lena Mills smiled. Sharon Richards sat in awe of what she had just heard. "Understood, Madam President." The name Liz just didn't seem to fit the occasion. "We're on the same wavelength, but I have a few questions," Sharon added. "How do you know these terrorists are U.S. citizens?"

"I'll get to that in a minute," the president answered.

"How am I supposed to do this? And what if I'm apprehended, either by authorities or the enemy?" Sharon asked, getting all of her questions out at once.

"You will have complete access to the same resources you've always had with your previous FBI position, as well as a 'top secret' clearance with the NSA and the other sixteen federal intelligence departments," Stanton answered. "Should you need assistance, you will also have the authority to recruit federal agents of your choosing. If anyone stands in your way, or if you need anything at all, call my secretary on her personal secure phone line, day or night. I will clear the way for you to proceed. Last, know that I will have your back...anonymously, of course. If anything goes wrong and your cover is blown, I can't promise you immunity from prosecution, but I can promise you a presidential pardon."

The president changed course. "You speak a number of Middle Eastern languages, including Arabic, do you not?"

"I'm a little rusty, but yes."

"Will Lambert says you have a few successful incursions under your belt."

"In Yemen and Saudi Arabia, but only briefly in each case to gather evidence."

"Then use your imagination. Terrorists hide behind veils, burqas and hijabs. You will as well."

Sharon still had a confused look on her face. "But why me? I still don't understand."

Stanton rose to pick up a file from the Resolute Desk. Handing one of the items in it to Sharon, the president sat again and waited, looking at Lena for approval. Lena was staring at Sharon, chuckling silently. *She's in for a surprise.*

Opening what she recognized as a Yemeni passport, Sharon gasped. The image of the woman could have been her own. "This is why," Stanton answered. "You're holding one of Malak al-Insaf's forged passports..."

"The 'Angel of Justice,' I know," Sharon interrupted. "She was a well-known al-Qaeda operative, an expert in explosives. But she died last year from a drone strike in northwest Waziristan. It was a confirmed kill."

"Yes, but we recovered her passports and other valuable information in the saddlebag of a donkey that was unharmed by the drone strike. Are you beginning to get the picture?"

"You want me to impersonate an internationally known terrorist who's believed to be dead?"

Lena could hold her silence no longer. "Bingo!" she exclaimed. "This woman is catching on fast, Liz."

Sharon wasn't buying in just yet. "So, I'm supposed to travel to remote Muslim tribal areas where this 'Angel of Justice' is known to operate, convince everyone that I'm not dead and just blend in?"

The president shook her head. "No, you will stay here in the states, where few people know you, but many know *of* you, and 'blend in,' as you say.

"Now, to answer your question. From audio surveillance, we're pretty sure the major players of these attacks operate out of a Brooklyn mosque. And we think the leader is the imam, a naturalized American citizen, Mustafa Shabbah. That's where you will infiltrate, gain his confidence, learn their plans and give us the names of as many players as possible." She handed Sharon the folder marked "TOP SECRET."

"I will let you borrow this dossier on Malak al-Insaf, with the understanding that it must be returned to Lena in two days. It covers her childhood until her death last year. I ask that you study this woman and memorize all her affiliations, kills, her lover who was also killed in the attack, even her personal quirks. When you meet with this imam, be bold and arrogant to convince him of your identity. If you can gain his confidence, you should be treated like a rock star back from the dead. Offer Shabbah your assistance in planning future attacks. Tell him you're here to avenge your lover's death. Because of your reputation, he should jump at the chance to work with you.

"Two more things," the president added. "You will read about these in the dossier, but we think they will seal the deal with the imam. This Angel of Justice was born in the U.S. of an American mother, which makes her a citizen. Second, Imam Shabbah and her Egyptian father were childhood friends. The imam knew Malak as a child by her

Americanized name, 'Malie.' In turn, she called the imam 'Uncle Baba.'"

President Stanton paused to let her last statements sink in. "As for compensation..."

Sharon interrupted. "I'm not concerned about compensation, Liz, but I do have two more concerns. Even if I'm successful and get you names, they'll likely be American citizens as well. We'll still have to arrest these homegrown terrorists and have them tried in a U.S. court of law."

Stanton glanced at Lena, who replied, "Not if they just...disappear." She paused for emphasis. "Please note that the president didn't say that. I did."

Sharon frowned but directed her last question to Lena. "Just what is your role in all of this?"

"Liz and I go back to when she was a fledgling South Carolina politician and I was the Florida governor's fiancé. We trust each other implicitly and we're in lockstep politically. If you choose to do this, I'll be your consultant and contact for this mission. Keeping you off the radar throughout the operation will be a top priority. If a problem arises, I will bullshit the press, something I've done with great success for decades.

"And, if need be, at sixty-five I can still kick ass," Lena added with a grin.

Sharon nodded. "I bet you can." Turning back to the president, she added, "Last thing. Because I lost my family, yet survived the cruise ship attack without injury, I've become some kind of pitiful celebrity. The press is after me. So far I've refused to comment..."

Lena broke in. "Then we must make you disappear, and I know just how to do it."

President Stanton rose from her chair and offered her hand. "Sharon, let me put all the cards on the table. What I'm asking you to do is legally out-of-bounds. If you're discovered, captured or killed, I will refuse to acknowledge your existence. I must have plausible deniability. On behalf of your country and as a personal favor to me, I beg you to consider this assignment seriously and quickly.

"I have other appointments now, but please inform Ms. Mills with your answer within two days at the latest." Stanton rose and offered her hand. "It was a pleasure meeting you, Sharon Richards. Lena, you can take it from here."

Sharon's headache had disappeared, replaced by an adrenaline high, as she followed Lena out of the Oval Office. Passing by Madelyn Forsyth's desk, Lena took Sharon aside. "Three days ago, you were enjoying life with your family, on the way to a wonderful vacation. Now your family is gone and you've been asked by the President of the United States to risk your life for your country. You must feel like the weight of the world has just been dumped on your shoulders."

"I want to help, but what should I do?" Sharon asked. Her whole body was shaking. "I'm not as strong or as confident as you."

Lena grasped her in a hug and held on until the shaking stopped. "How did you get here?" she asked.

"I hired a ride from Philadelphia. My driver is waiting to take me back home."

"I don't have to tell you that this dossier needs to be guarded with your life. Read, study and memorize everything about this woman. She was some piece of work. As the president said, you must return this to me with your answer within two days. I'm staying at the Hay-Adams Hotel near here. Please return it in person with your answer. With something this important, I don't trust couriers, phone conversations, e-mails or handwritten notes."

Sharon looked into Lena's piercing eyes and nodded in agreement.

Lena gripped both of Sharon's arms. "You remind me of my best friend, Anne Henderson. She was blessed with a mystical power that baffled her. When she died of brain cancer at a young age, her spirit continued to communicate with me. Without elaborating the details, from that point on, I was also blessed...or cursed, some might say...with a power that allowed me to do things that made me famous. Things like take on Congress and the President of the United States that I could not have done by myself. So my strong, confident reputation is highly overrated."

"What does your life have to do with mine?" asked Sharon.

Lena withdrew her hands and stepped aside. "I can sense it, hon. Compared to what is being asked of you, my crusade against political corruption was minor. But, along the way, I learned that there are two kinds of people—those that talk and those who do. From what I've read and seen of you today, I'm sure you're the latter.

"Inside you is a strength you don't understand. Don't fight it, use it. Coupled with your desire for revenge, I'd hate to be your adversary." She gave Sharon another quick hug. "Now go. Study the dossier. Two days, no more, okay?"

Exhausted, Sharon walked out of the North Portico and called for her driver. When the limousine arrived, she lay back and closed her eyes, looking forward to the three-hour drive to Philadelphia. Within two minutes, she was fast asleep. Assaulting her slumber were memories of falling, frigid water, a gigantic fireball, gasping for air—and that damned poem.

Do not go gentle into that good night, Rage, rage against the dying of the light.

21

SUPER 8 MOTEL
LAS VEGAS, NEVADA
NOON

"PHASE TWO." The gruff voice on the iPhone added, "Download and copy the manifest. Execute at five p.m. *Insha'Allah*."

Mehrala al-Haq looked at his partner, Ashami Najar. "We must wait until four to do our last preparations. Asha, move the truck into some shade. We must not let the cargo get too hot. It might explode."

Najar left the comfort of their motel room and hurried to the huge truck. With the outside temperature at ninety-eight degrees and climbing, the cab was stifling hot. Starting the truck, he immediately switched the air conditioner to "MAX." It took a minute for the cab temperature to reach seventy degrees.

At midday, the motel parking lot was nearly empty. Najar moved the truck under a bank of overhanging shade trees. He opened the back cab window, let the cool air work its way into the rear payload box, and waited.

Meanwhile, Mehrala downloaded the pirated Sysco manifest and printed a hard copy.

When Najar returned, Mehrala greeted him with, "What took you so long? Is something wrong?"

"No, but the cab was quite hot. I turned on the AC for ten minutes and made sure the back got cooled off. The shade will help, but just to make sure, we should do this every hour." Najar pointed to the printout in Mehrala's hand. "Is that the manifest?"

"Yes. I will arrive one hour before the real Sysco truck as planned. Now we wait."

22

CHESTNUT HILL, PENNSYLVANIA
3 P.M.

SHARON RICHARDS woke to the gentle prodding of her driver, Sam. She was covered in perspiration. "Ma'am, you're home. You've been asleep. Sounded like you were having nightmares all the way back," he added.

Groggy, she rose to a sitting position and grabbed the dossier, only to face flashing cameras and questions from reporters trying to invade the interior of the limo. Six-foot-seven Sam would have none of it. He brushed back the offending newshounds with a sweep of his huge forearm. "Out of the way," he shouted, ushering his client through the gauntlet of paparazzi to the house.

As Sharon opened her front door, Sam gave her a card with his personal number. "Give me a call anytime you need a ride, day or night, Mrs. Richards." She thanked him and quickly went inside. Taking a deep breath, she felt somewhat refreshed in spite of her troubled nap.

The home phone answering machine was blinking, jammed with messages. They could wait.

She poured herself a tall glass of water and began reading the dossier.

Hours later, Sharon came to three conclusions. First, although she was ten years older, she was almost identical physically in height, stature, hair and skin color, to the dead terrorist, Malak al-Insaf. Both were fluent in Arabic, Farsi and Persian, as well as English. This 'Angel of Justice' was also necessarily fluent in Pashto, the tribal dialect of Afghanistan and Pakistan. She had an extensive resume of death and destruction throughout the Middle East and those same tribal regions. Most important, she had not returned to the United States in over twenty-five years.

Second, Sharon's family was gone. *What else do I have to live for?* Something Lena Mills had said stuck in her mind. "We must make you disappear, and I know just how to do it."

And third...*I can do this.*

23

LAS VEGAS, NEVADA

MEHRALA DROVE to a nearby deserted parking lot. There, both men removed the temporary covers on each side of the truck, exposing blue "Good things come from Sysco" logos. The truck might be inspected, so they removed smaller covers from each drum inside the cargo bed, revealing the names of various cooking oils.

Ashami Najar looked at his watch. It read 4:15 p.m. "Let's go. By the time you drop me off at the motel and drive to Caesar's, it will be five."

At the motel, they hugged. "All is prepared, my brother," Najar whispered. "I am envious. Allah is waiting for you."

Tears flowed down Mehrala's cheeks. No other words were necessary. He got back into the truck, waved goodbye and drove away from his friend for the last time.

Unlike most major cities, rush hour in Las Vegas is typically between eight and ten a.m. Mehrala encountered no backed-up traffic at this time of the afternoon. He drove his truck down Las Vegas Boulevard, turned west on Sahara, then south on Industrial, which merged with Frank Sinatra Way.

Reaching the service drive for Caesar's Palace, he turned left and stopped at the gate.

"You're early," commented the guard as he compared Mehrala's Sysco manifest with his own. "Cooking oils," he grunted. Pointing to three large trucks waiting to unload their cargo, he added, "Line up behind those. When your turn comes, someone will flag you. Back into the dock so a forklift can unload your drums. You know the drill, right?"

Mehrala nodded and tried to look bored as he got in line. He dreaded the wait. *Allah is trying me*, he said to himself. *Patience! I must be patient.*

Thoughts of his mother came to mind. Fatima al-Haq had lost her husband during the South Lebanese conflict in 1978. Fleeing from the violence that tore her country apart, she successfully applied for emigration to the United States. Within three years, Fatima became a citizen. In 1991, feeling financially stable with a steady job in a textile mill, she adopted a newborn son in 1991. She named him Mehrala, in tribute to her grandfather. Mother and son settled in a Brooklyn, New York apartment. Gentle and kind Fatima would sing Lebanese songs of pain and sacrifice while rocking Mehrala to sleep in her arms. Some of the melodies still haunted his dreams.

A devout Muslim, Fatima enrolled her son in a local madrassa, thinking it would teach him basic moral values. Instead, he received rigid indoctrination in Wahhabism and sharia law.

During his formative years, Mehrala memorized the Qur'an and laws of Islamic fundamentalism. By the time he was a teenager, he was ripe for recruitment. At age eighteen, he was sent to a remote region of Pakistan and trained in combat techniques, mental toughness and unquestioned loyalty to jihad. The last few years in Syria, he had killed and maimed many in Bashar Assad's army. It was there he learned of an American spiritual leader, an imam named Shabbah, who was determined destroy the Great Satan.

Entering the U.S. again, Mehrala became a member of Imam Shabbah's army of terror. It was then he met Dr. Abu Mazra, the jihad mastermind and befriended another warrior, an illegal immigrant from Syria, Ashami Najar. Since Mehrala was the senior of the two, he drew the honor of this day's self-sacrifice.

Mehrala al-Haq looked at his watch. It read 4:55. A man was waving his hands, gesturing for him to back into the loading dock. *This is it.*

Taking a deep breath, he put the large truck in reverse and let the idle take it backward. Mehrala was a few feet from the dock when he saw a guard approaching. At the guard's side was a leashed German shepherd.

All thoughts and memories vanished with a rush of panic. Reaching for his iPhone, Mehrala pushed "SEND" and screamed.

24

HAVING MADE up her mind, Sharon resolved to inform Lena of her decision personally the next day. Her stomach growled, reminding her that she had not eaten anything since an early breakfast. She made a sandwich, filled a glass with water and took both back to the living room.

Sharon turned on the television. At first, she thought the scenes of mass devastation were recaps of the airplane assaults four days ago. When she realized they were new, Sharon ignored her sandwich, grabbed Sam's card and dialed the number. Forgetting to announce her name when he answered, she blurted out, "You said anytime day or night. I need you, Sam. Please come back and pick me up. I'll pay you double this time."

She had enough time to pack a few things, write a check and a letter, and take a quick shower. Sharon blew off the two reporters who remained in her yard and ran next door. Hearing the chime, Phyllis Schumacher opened her front door. The woman she had last seen two days ago—home from the hospital, in pain, drawn, in mourning—bore no resemblance to the woman standing in front of her today. The old Sharon

119

Richards, the FBI Agent Sharon Richards Phyllis had known for many years, was now a picture of confidence...and in a hurry.

"Hi, Sharon. Have you seen...?"

"Please, Phyllis," Sharon interrupted. "I only have a few minutes. We need to talk. Please get Ken, if he's available."

Phyllis gestured for her to come inside and called for her husband, who hugged Sharon. "I'm so sorry..." he began.

"Thanks, Ken, but I don't have much time. My ride will be here at any minute." She looked at both of her dear neighbors, wondering where to begin. *Just begin at the beginning,* she chastised herself. *You're in a hurry, so get it over with.*

"I'm going away. I don't know how long or if I'll ever come back. Please believe I would tell you more, but I can't."

Phyllis began to cry. "Oh, hon..."

Sharon grabbed her in a fierce hug and held on. "You two have been the best friends we could ever hope for, but now I have to ask you both a favor."

"Anything," Ken answered.

"Look after the house. Treat it and use it as your own. Contact the woman who was here two days ago when I came home from the hospital. Her name is Gloria Hyde." She handed the house key and an envelope to Ken. "Her number and address are inside. Gloria works at a law firm that acts as our...my trustee. The letter inside instructs her firm to pay all bills, repairs and taxes on the house when they come due, and to give you anything else you need regarding the house."

A horn honked outside. "This must be my ride. I'm sorry I can't be any more candid, other than to say how much I appreciate your kindness all these years. There's something inside the envelope that expresses my appreciation."

By now Phyllis was bawling. Ken had a bewildered look on his face. Sharon, on the verge of tears herself, ended with a brief hug for both. "Gotta go now. I may or may not be in touch."

With that, she left both neighbors staring after her, as she handed over a single suitcase and a briefcase to her driver, climbed in the limo and was gone.

Phyllis was still in tears when Ken opened the envelope. Sure enough, there was a letter addressed to Gloria Hyde...and a check for $200,000, payable to Ken and Phyllis Schumacher.

Ken reeled in shock. "Holy Mother of Jesus!"

"What is it?" Phyllis asked, reaching for the letter and check. Seeing the amount, she gasped and sank into the nearest chair.

25

**THE WHITE HOUSE
SITUATION ROOM
9 P.M.**

SURROUNDED BY ten of the most powerful people in the country, President Elizabeth Stanton remained silent while the bickering in the Situation Room continued to escalate. Instead, she watched in horror as scenes of looting, vandalism, and random violence played out on the major television networks.

Four hours ago, three coordinated truck bombings had leveled huge sections of the Mall of America in Minnesota, Caesar's Palace Resort in Las Vegas, and the Fontainebleau Resort in Miami Beach. Local police and National Guard divisions were assisting fire and emergency personnel, who were doing their best to control each scene. Most were overwhelmed by the sheer number of anarchists who raised random havoc with bats, knives and guns.

Recovery teams continued to search through rubble in San Francisco, Chicago and New York Bay for possible survivors from the airplane assaults four days earlier. Those events now seemed like ancient history. The press continued to stoke the fires of unrest, interviewing countless bloodied survivors and capturing scenes of police wielding batons and spraying tear gas against brazen lawbreakers. Panning across a sea of rubble and severed body parts in Miami Beach, one television anchor wailed, "Oh, the inhumanity! Is this the end of America?"

Disgusted, Stanton stood and clicked off the master television remote. As she gestured for calm, all conversation came to an abrupt halt. "Our country is coming apart at the seams," she began. "Is there a doubt in anyone's mind that these truck bombings and the airplane attacks came from the same cell of domestic terrorists?"

Seeing no disagreement, Stanton continued. Addressing General Stanley McElhinney of the NSA, she asked, "Stan, exactly what do we have on this Brooklyn mosque group?"

"Madam President, we have numerous conversations between the imam, a fellow named Shabbah, and members of his mosque. Some are quite suggestive but none is conclusive. Of particular interest is one conversation that took place inside the mosque a couple hours before the airplane attacks. It was picked up and recorded by one of our operatives outside, using a parabolic microphone, and copied onto this."

McElhinney pulled a flash drive from his briefcase and inserted it into his computer. "The first voice belongs to Imam Shabbah," the general explained. *'Have you received confirmation? Is everyone in place?'*

"This second voice has not been identified."

'Yes, imam.'

'And what of the principals?'

'All are on schedule and prepared. There are no delays, and the conditions are ideal, Insha'Allah.'

McElhinney broke in, "And here are the most interesting two sentences. They are spoken by the imam: '*We will only get one chance at this before countermeasures are taken. Muhammad, my son, if Allah blesses us this day, your name will live forever.*'"

The general looked up and added, "While we do not know who this other fellow is, from the conversation we can assume that the person named 'Muhammad' is one of the leaders, if not *the* leader, of this gang of terrorists."

The Secretary of Defense, Dale Eggars, broke in. "If your people were outside listening to the conversation, didn't anyone take pictures of everyone entering and exiting the mosque at that time?"

"Yes, of course, Mr. Secretary. We ran facial recognition on all seventy-seven men who entered the mosque that day. A few are on the Terrorist Watch List. The women were dressed in hijabs and burqas, used the side entrance and were impossible to identify."

Eggars followed with another question. "Why hasn't this mosque been assaulted by the public, unlike so many others?"

"There were two attempts in the last three days," explained McElhinney."Both were thwarted by seven of the men I mentioned, each armed to the teeth. This mosque is like a nest of hornets, ready to swarm anyone who threatens it."

General Jablonsky rose to his feet. "I say we storm the place and arrest this imam," he shouted. "He's obviously a ringleader. We should stop pussyfooting around and..."

"And what, general?" the president interrupted. "Torture the guy? Don't be ridiculous. You know he'd lawyer up faster than greased lightning, and then where would we be? He'd know that we're onto him and we would never be able to locate any of his operatives."

Madelyn Forsyth had entered the room during the last heated exchange. Approaching Stanton, she placed a note next to the president and glided from the room with the grace of a ballerina.

Jablonsky's eyes followed Forsyth out the door. "Do you have a better idea?" he challenged the president.

Stanton looked at the note. A slight smile creased her lips. "Maybe I do."

With that the president marched out of the Situation Room, leaving her national defense team to argue among themselves.

26

LENA MILLS answered the phone. After a lengthy discussion, she thanked the caller, hung up and returned to the living room. Sharon Richards had arrived about thirty minutes earlier. Lena introduced her to two large men, explaining only that her guest was a survivor of the cruise ship attack four days ago.

"That was Madelyn Forsyth. She has relayed your message to the president," Lena told Sharon, taking her aside. Using the remote, she turned on the large screen television and pushed the MUTE button, then sat next to her husband, Cal Carpenter. A former Marine, Secret Service agent and U.S. Marshal before retiring to serve as Lena's personal bodyguard, he had saved her life during one of two assassination attempts. A missing joint on his left thumb was proof of his devotion.

Lena pointed to the TV screen which was split into the three major networks plus FOX. All four showed scenes of devastation and rioting from the three truck explosions. "Liz is going to address the nation again at ten."

"What's she going to say? The country's going to hell and I quit?" snapped the other man in his deep bass voice. Seventy-five-year-old Claude Masters was Lena's oldest and closest friend. In 1968, she had been hired as a stripper at an Orlando gentlemen's club. Claude was the club's bouncer. Over the next few years, as Lena's fame grew and she became the toast of Central Florida nightlife, Claude was her personal bodyguard, workout partner, confidant and critic.

Following Lena's skyrocketing career as a media superstar and political pundit, Claude was always at her side, making sarcastic comments while watching her back. Theirs was a strange relationship of insults and mutual admiration that had stood the test of time.

Lena scowled at her friend of forty-plus years. "I just hung up with the president's personal secretary. According to Madelyn Forsyth, the NSA and FBI think they have a lead on this terrorist cell. The president needs to buy time while this lead is confirmed, so she's placing all U.S. metropolitan areas with a population over a million under temporary martial law.

"And no," Lena added, pointing at Claude, "there's not an ounce of quit in Elizabeth Stanton."

Claude snorted. "Is she serious? With this woman in charge, we've gone from a representative democracy to a police state, no better than Cuba."

Gesturing at Sharon, he asked, "Excuse me, little lady, but exactly why are you here?"

Lena bristled at his rude question. "Claude Masters, if you weren't so old and crotchety, I'd take you over my knee and whup your black hide!"

"You and who else?" he retorted with a grin. "I can still tan your skinny white ass, and don't you forget it."

Sharon opened her mouth to speak but said nothing. Fascinated with the playful pissing contest, she forgot the hell she had been through, forgot that she was in mourning for her family...and giggled.

"Don't mind them," Cal said, looking at Sharon. "Neither of these geriatric brats has ever grown up. Lena tells me you're FBI."

Sharon looked at Lena before answering. "Yes sir, but I retired a little while ago."

Cal pointed to himself. "Secret Service and U.S. Marshal, before my feisty wife rescued me from government service."

"You were on the presidential detail for five years, credited with saving the life of a Supreme Court justice, and your father was a Medal of Honor recipient," Sharon replied. "On the way here, I've been studying Lena's history on the net...as well as yours, sir," she explained.

Cal smiled. "Drop the 'sir.' No need to make me feel any older than I am."

"I apologize, young lady," Claude broke in. "Whatever your reason for being here, if Lena says you're okay, that's enough for me."

"No apology necessary, Mr. Masters," Sharon said with a smile. "I'm sorry, but I can't disclose why I'm here, at least for the time being. It's classified."

Cal stared at Claude as if to say, "Butt out." He turned to Lena. "I can see why you like this president. She's just like you—lead, follow, or get the hell out of the way."

Claude shook his head in silence, looking like he just swallowed a whole prune—pit and all.

Lena switched off the television and pointed to the door. "It's bedtime, Claude. Get some sleep and don't worry. The sun will come up tomorrow just like it did today."

Cal ushered her grumbling friend out the door, returned to kiss his wife and shake Sharon's hand. "I'm going to bed, too. I'll leave you both to talk."

Lena pulled out a bed from the room's convertible sofa. "This is very comfortable. I use it sometimes when Cal snores." She shook her head, put her hands on Sharon's shoulders and smiled. "Two trips to Washington, meeting with the president, deciding to risk your life for your country—I'd say you've had one hell of a day."

Sharon yawned. "Now that you mention it, I am exhausted."

"Get some sleep, girl. Tomorrow, Sharon Richards will cease to exist. I'm going to turn you into a dead woman."

DAY FIVE

27

STATEN ISLAND, NEW YORK
SATURDAY, 7 A.M.

DR. ABU MAZRA'S upper lip curled in disgust, watching his assistant Firouz Ahmed address the roomful of twenty-two eager followers. All recruits were disaffected young American men who had pledged their allegiance and lives to Allah and were thoroughly indoctrinated in Islamic law. Most had driven non-stop to New York for this meeting. Parking their rental cars in the mosque's lot, each operative had taken an MTA bus to a stop near this clandestine meeting place—an old warehouse in an abandoned Staten Island marine salvage yard. To avoid suspicion, all took care to arrive in small groups or separately.

Absent were three team members, martyrs who had already sacrificed their lives in the truck bombings for the glory of Allah. They would find their rewards in Heaven.

Three of these soldiers, including Ashami Najar, had performed their support duties in the truck bombings to perfection, thanks to the professor's iron-willed discipline and Ahmed's ingenuity and faultless attention to detail. The rest had been trained well, but as yet not seen direct action.

Flush with satisfaction that his training sessions had yielded maximum results, Ahmed was congratulating each of the three support jihadists for a job well done. Abu Mazra felt that praise was unnecessary, indeed a sign of weakness. It was time to put his young protégé in his place.

The professor raised his hands and nudged him aside. "Enough!" He looked askance at Ahmed, who was fuming with embarrassment. "Always look forward," he ordered, pointing at the younger man for emphasis, "never backward."

Ignoring Ahmed's daggered stare, Abu Mazra continued. "We will let our crippling attacks fester with the infidels for a week. They fear our next move and are rebelling against their hapless leaders. Protests and riots in the streets increase every day. There are calls for presidential impeachment. Like all women, Stanton is a weak and spineless leader—all talk and no action. What is her response to the chaos we have created? The gutless bitch has ordered martial law and imposed useless curfews."

One hand went up, vying for attention. Annoyed at the interruption, the professor nodded in the owner's direction. "Dr. Abu Mazra, we are eager for action. What do you have planned for us with Phase Three?"

"Be patient," chastised the professor. He paused to scan each eager face. "We will meet here in four days, again at seven a.m. It is an ideal time because no one else will be anywhere this place, for obvious reasons." In a rare moment of levity, he pretended to pinch his nose closed, which drew a few chuckles from his followers.

"At that meeting, I will reveal the plan and we can begin preparing weapons for our next phase, which will include all of you.

"Picture a cat toying with a mouse before the kill. The great and all-powerful Allah is the cat and we are His teeth and claws. America is in our grasp, wiggling helplessly. Victory is at hand. *Allahu Akbar!*"

Rising to their feet, the army of al-Qaeda in America raised their fists and shouted as one, *"Alhamdulillah!"*

28

WASHINGTON, D.C.
NOON

TWO MIDDLE-AGED WOMEN, one blonde and one brunette, strode forth from the Hay-Adams Hotel. Both looked slightly overweight and seemed to be in their mid-sixties. Elegantly dressed, each carried a large tote bag.

Hailing a cab, the blonde barked out a destination. "What's your name, son?" she asked the driver, staring at his image in the rearview mirror. The young man looked to be in his twenties and wore a turban.

"Call me Raj," he replied with a sing-song accent. Looking at Lena in the mirror, he smiled.

"You have a family, Raj?"

"Yes, ma'am. Wife and three children."

Lena smiled back at his mirror image and held up a wad of cash. "If I offer you a thousand dollars, can we rent your services until five and you keep your mouth shut while we talk?"

"Most surely. Definitely. Of course," Raj blubbered, pleased with his good fortune.

Lena counted out five hundred-dollar bills and put them into the young man's outstretched hand. "Half now and the other half at five, okay?"

"Most surely!" Raj repeated, turning off his meter and waiting for instructions.

Lena turned to Sharon. "When's the last time you had a girl's day out?"

"I can't remember when...or even if."

To avoid recognition, they had spent the last two hours in Lena's suite experimenting with a disguise, something simple that Sharon could easily apply. The result was an understated head-to-toe transformation, from a lean, all-business, thirty-something look, to a wealthy, sixty-something society matron.

Changing into her own "Lumpy" disguise was second nature to Lena. In her twenties and thirties as a famous stripper in Orlando's classiest nightclub, she had used it countless times to ward off gawkers and the press. Throwing on a wig, tucking into her bodice strategically placed padding under a stylish matronly dress and applying a few strokes of makeup and toned-down lipstick, took slightly more than three minutes.

"Should we begin rehearsing now or wait?" Sharon asked, wondering where they were going.

"At lunch would be best. We've got all afternoon. Let's try to have some fun, shall we? I haven't been out with a girlfriend since..." She paused, tearing up at the thought.

Sharon was caught off guard by Lena's abrupt mood change. "What's the matter?"

"Just a flashback, dear. Ancient history. I was thinking of my best friend, Anne Henderson. It was so long ago..."

"The one who died of brain cancer and gave you some kind of mental power, right?"

Lena nodded and grasped Sharon's hand. "Like you, I've lost loved ones. Two hit me the hardest, Anne and her daughter—

my adopted niece—Tracy. At my age, it seems everyone has lost someone close. What makes it worse for both of us is how we lost them—suddenly and tragically."

Sharon refused to lapse into another episode of self-pity. "I remember reading about Tracy. You were onstage when someone tried to shoot you. The bullet hit her instead."

Lena stared ahead and nodded again, tears streaming down her face.

"I'm sorry. I shouldn't have…"

"It's okay, dear," Lena answered, blowing her nose on a Kleenex. "I haven't had a good cry in ages, but I must look a mess. My make-up…"

Sharon handed Lena a compact mirror and more Kleenex. "Nothing a few of these can't cure."

The ten-mile drive to College Park took less than thirty minutes. Stopping at an outlet that specialized in Muslim clothing, Sharon bought a multi-colored bundle of five hijab caps, two slip-on kaftan kurtis—one blue and one black, a pair of comfortable flats and a full-length burqa, should one be needed for formal occasions.

As Sharon and Lena came out of the store, Raj wondered what two elderly American women would want with traditional Muslim garb, but he followed instructions and asked no questions.

Lena looked at Sharon with raised eyebrows. "Let me guess. You're not a fan of exotic food, right?"

"I do prefer good old meat and potatoes," she answered, "but you know the DC area. I can eat anything."

"Take us to the Monocle Restaurant, Raj," Lena ordered the eager face in the rearview mirror. Turning back to Sharon, she added. "It's quiet. We can talk all afternoon."

Over a light lunch, Lena used the dossier on thirty-year-old Malak al-Insaf to grill Sharon on everything from the female terrorist's demeanor, habits and history, to her portfolio of bombings and affiliations. After two hours of intense questioning, Lena put down the file. "You're ready."

"Two things bother me about this mission," Sharon confessed. "I'm fifty, and this woman was thirty. Even if I do resemble this woman, do you really think I can pull off impersonating someone twenty years younger?"

"Hon, in your case, fifty is the new thirty. Believe me, I should know. You're a hot babe and I'm jealous."

Sharon laughed. "Must be that extra martini talking. In these disguises, anyone hearing us talk would think we're two batty old broads ready for the loony bin."

"What's the second thing?" Lena asked.

"My fluency in Middle Eastern languages is a little rusty. What if I have to converse at length..."

"I'm guessing everyone you'll meet is either a citizen by birth or naturalized," Lena interrupted. "Just rehearse an opening line for the imam and you should be using English from then on. And remember...be bold. Don't let anyone intimidate you. I know you can handle this. Just think of your mission. You'll be fine."

Lena pulled a cell phone out of her bag and handed it to Sharon. "Just in case, here's your lifeline. It has the latest encrypted technology. There are only two numbers programmed in speed dial—mine and the president's personal secretary. You met Madelyn. Call her and she will put you through to Liz immediately."

She rose from the booth and picked up the check. "Let's get out of here. We've still got to rent you a car and an apartment. You'll also need enough cash for the next two weeks, at least."

Sharon grabbed the check out of Lena's hand. "Lunch is on me, and I've got plenty of cash."

"Look, babe, I'm loaded, and I don't mean with liquor," argued Lena. "And, I'm getting reimbursed by the government. You're a civilian who has volunteered to lay your life on the line for your country. The least it can do is pay for your lunch."

Shaking her head in resignation, Sharon relinquished her grip on the check. *If she only knew...*

DAY SIX

29

BROOKLYN, NEW YORK
SUNDAY, 3 P.M.

SHE HAD PLANNED to arrive at the end of salat. Nearly all worshippers had left the mosque when Sharon parked her rental car and approached the front door. Dressed in her blue kaftan kurti and decorative hijab cap, she was blocked from entering by a much taller man with a hostile glare. Obviously one of the building's guards, the man spoke in an authoritative voice, "Women must use the side entrance. No exceptions."

"I wish to speak with your spiritual leader, Imam Shabbah," Sharon stated, meeting the man's stern gaze with her own.

The man grabbed her arm and began to lead her down the entrance stairway. "The imam does not meet with unaccompanied…"

With lightning speed, Sharon shook off the guard's grasp and smashed the palm of one hand into his jaw, while planting a vice-grip on his crotch with the other. As he staggered, she hissed, "The last man who grabbed me like that died…painfully. Now, what'll it be? An audience with the imam, or more of this?"

Sharon viciously wrenched the man's testicles, bringing him to his knees, screaming, "Okay, okay, pleeeaase! No more!"

She released her grip on the victim, who collapsed into a fetal position, holding his privates and moaning in pain. Hearing the commotion, another guard appeared, looking confused as he stared at his prostrate colleague and the much smaller woman standing over him. Since the first guard was hopelessly preoccupied, Sharon pointed to the other. "Tell Imam Shabbah that Malie wishes to see her Uncle Baba...now!"

The second guard hesitated a second before disappearing through the entrance door. Hearing the ruckus, two more curious guards came from the building's side entrance, then two more. The four circled Sharon and her prostate victim. As they moved in to tackle the offending interloper, the front door opened.

A tall, imposing man resembling Charlton Heston's Moses looked over the scene and motioned his guards to step aside. "I am Imam Mustafa Shabbah. Who are you?" he demanded, looming over Sharon with a stern look. "Only one person has ever dared to call me Uncle Baba, and she is dead."

From a pocket in her tunic, Sharon slowly pulled out her alter ego's American passport and handed it to the imam without comment. Imam Shabbah put on his glasses and stared at the picture, then put it next to Sharon's face, comparing the image. Waiting a few seconds to see if she would flinch, he shook his head. "You cannot be Malie."

Instead of arguing, Sharon kneeled before the imam and recited a Muslim chant that, according to the dossier, the imam had made the young girl memorize a quarter century earlier. *"La ilaha illa Allah al Halim al Karim. La ilaha illa Allah al `Aliyy al `Athim. Subhanallahi Rabbi samawati sab` wa Rabb*

146

al aradina sab` wa ma fi hinna wa ma bayna hunna, wa Rabbil `arsh al `athim. Wal hamdu lillahi Rabbil `alamin. There is no god but Allah, the Forbearing, the Generous. There is no god but Allah, the Eminent, the Great. Glory be to Allah, the Sustainer of the seven heavens and of the seven earths, the Sustainer of all the things in them, and between them, the Lord of the great Throne. And praise be to Allah, the Lord of the worlds."

Imam Shabbah beamed with pride. "You *are* alive!" he cried, taking her in his long arms. "*Alhamdulillah!* Praise be to Allah!"

Except for the hapless guard still on the ground writhing in pain, the remaining guards looked confused. Who was this stranger? Why was she here?

Ignoring them, the imam guided Sharon into the mosque, down a hallway and into his private quarters, where he hugged her again, offered a chair and put a finger to his lips. During the walk, she slipped a hand inside her tunic to make sure her slim pen digital audio recorder was still on.

"Your imam is a hugger," Lena had told Sharon before she left on her mission. "He hugs his parishioners all the time. Instead of wearing a wire that he can easily feel under your tunic, take this pen. It looks and writes just like any ballpoint, but it's also a very sensitive digital recorder that can pick up sound, even under your loose-fitting top."

Shabbah put a finger to his lips and cautioned, "We must talk softly. **The enemy is most certainly listening.**" He continued in a voice barely more than a whisper. "After all these years...I've heard and read so many things about you.

You're known throughout Islam as 'The Sword of Allah'; 'Bomb-maker of the jihad...'"

"Names," Sharon interrupted with a muted voice, gaining confidence with the imam's apparent acceptance. "Names mean nothing. Pursuing the glory of Allah is everything. You and my father taught me this."

"But how did you survive the drone attack?" he asked. "You are supposed to be dead."

"*Insha'Allah*. It was God's will," Sharon replied. "I had just exited the tent when the bomb hit. I was far enough away from the blast to survive with only a few scratches. I was deaf for two days." She bowed her head. "My lover was inside and did not survive. *Inna lilahi wa inna Ilaehi Rajiun*. May God rest his soul."

The imam reached out and held her hand. "*Amin*. So be it."

Sharon looked around the imam's sparsely decorated sanctuary. "Can we go somewhere to talk—somewhere you aren't being monitored?"

Shabbah shook his head and whispered, "I am a self-imposed prisoner in my own mosque. I dare not leave for fear of being detained by the infidels. I am sure the government suspects that I have something to do with these recent attacks."

Sharon leaned forward for emphasis. "My sources tell me that this is true. That is why I have come."

Smiling, the imam changed the subject. "How did you get into the country? You must also be on the 'Watch List.'"

Sharon returned his smile and shook her head. "This country's borders are a joke. Anyone with an ounce of imagination can cross the southern border and disappear. In case I need them, I also have forged passports and other identification with a number of aliases." She leaned back in the chair. "Besides, as you rightly said, I am supposed to be dead."

Imam Shabbah bored in with more questions. "Tell me, child, what happened to your parents when you left America? I lost touch with your father, my childhood friend. It was in 1985, was it not?"

Sharon hesitated. *He's testing me.* "You must be getting old, Imam Shabbah, it was 1990 and I was five," she answered. "My parents took me to your country of birth, Egypt, to join the Muslim Brotherhood and fight against Mubarak, but my father was gunned down like a dog by the Mabahith Amn ad-Dawla, the Egyptian Secret Service. Mother wanted to bring me back home to America, but her passport had been revoked because of Father's Brotherhood affiliation.

"So we escaped to Lebanon, where we were refugees without a country. Arafat took us in and that is where we lived for many years. In 1997, when I was twelve, Mother became ill with pneumonia and died. Throughout my teenage years, I trained as an apprentice to Awad al-Qiq, the Palestinian bomb-maker. Later, I trained under the Egyptian, Abu Abdul Rahman a-Muhajir. Since I left Lebanon at the age of twenty, I have moved from country to country, selling my skills to the highest bidder and have built a reputation of my own."

Sharon paused, looking for any sign of doubt on the imam's face. During her historical summary, she noticed the man nodding in recognition of the infamous bomb-makers—a good sign. "Over the last decade, I have made sophisticated devices with maximum killing power. If you'll have me, I am here to offer my assistance to you and your followers."

Over the next hour, the two freely exchanged questions and answers. Finally, Imam Shabbah had heard enough. Standing, he embraced his adopted niece once again and whispered into her ear, "You have brought honor to your Muslim name, Malak al-Insaf. You are indeed the 'Angel of Justice!'"

It took all of Sharon's will power to withstand each of the imam's embraces. The urge to end his life immediately was tempting. This was a holy man who pretended to preach love, compassion and tolerance in his daily khutbas, all the while plotting to murder thousands of innocent people—a man who, in the name of his deity, felt no remorse in subverting a religion for his evil cause.

In her mind, guilt and rationalization played out in a game of emotional ping-pong. *I'm plotting to murder as well. Am I any better than this man?*

But saving the lives of thousands is my cause, her mind answered.

Don't kid yourself, she argued. *You know that's not the real reason you're here. Let your pent-up anger destroy this madman and his brotherhood of killers!*

As she pulled away from the imam's embrace, Sharon's expression turned dark with rage. She growled with all the venom she could muster. "But we know why I'm really here, don't we? I have returned to avenge my lover's death!"

Imam Shabbah picked up a cell phone and pushed an automatic dial button. After two rings, someone answered. Without greeting, he ordered in a soft but firm voice, "I am sending a woman to meet with you at your office, eleven a.m.

tomorrow. She will announce herself as Malie. Do not question her loyalty or credentials. She has come from overseas to help us. Give her anything she needs and include her in the preparations for Phase Three."

Without waiting for an answer, the imam disconnected. He opened his desk and pulled out another cell phone and handed it to Sharon. This is a secure line that is programmed directly to me. All of our phones are encrypted with the latest technology and routed through servers around the world.

The imam wrote some instructions on a slip of paper and handed it to her. "Go to this address at eleven tomorrow," he whispered. "It's the Graduate Center of the City College of New York.' He pointed to a name. "Find this man's office. He is vain and irascible, and if he gives you any trouble, call me. My number is on speed dial."

Sharon hesitated before accepting the phone. *It looks just like the one Lena gave me.*

"Never speak this man's name," the imam continued. "He is the coordinator of our jihad and invaluable to our cause. He will introduce you to my soldiers of Allah. Use all your knowledge and skills to enhance our plans, for it is this team of dedicated followers who will make your revenge possible."

Sharon looked at the name on the piece of paper and whispered, "I've heard of this man. Isn't he a famous scientist?"

Imam Mustafa Shabbah put a cautionary finger to his lips, beaming with pride. "Nobel Prize famous."

30

HAY-ADAMS HOTEL
7 P.M.

LENA MILLS sat on the living room couch, watching the suite's large screen television, muted so she could brood to Mahler's Ninth Symphony. Cal knew to leave her alone when she was in "one of her moods," so was in the hotel lobby playing cribbage with Claude. She answered her cell phone on the first ring. No acknowledgments were necessary. "I've been on pins and needles for hours," Lena barked. "The waiting is driving me crazy. Where the hell have you been?"

Sharon deflected the question. "How secure is this phone?"

"You have to ask? Please!"

"Sorry. The imam gave me one, too. Now I've got two phones that look exactly alike."

"Put a tiny sticker on one of them," Lena suggested. "Now, spill!"

Over the next half-hour, Sharon described the meeting with Shabbah, omitting her emotions. She ended with, "After the meeting, I was hungry and found a cheap diner and pigged out on comfort food. I didn't want to call you from the car or restaurant."

Lena was ecstatic. "Okay, I forgive you. Great job! Did you get names?"

"Yes, some, but don't mention anything specific to YKW until I meet with the coordinator tomorrow." Lena and Sharon had agreed never to mention the president by name. Instead, they would refer to her as YKW, an acronym for "you-know-who."

Sharon's trust in encrypted phone technology came with a healthy dose of skepticism. "How are you holding up? What's new from your end?"

"I've been getting calls from Madelyn for updates. Have you seen the news?"

Sharon had been watching the television in her room. Protests, many turning into riots, were now commonplace all over the world. If the most powerful nation on earth couldn't protect itself, no country was safe from harm.

Here at home, outraged protesters were taking to the streets in greater numbers, ignoring the president's pleas for calm. Strident calls for her impeachment from members of Congress were increasing by the hour. On a split screen, remains of the bombed buildings reduced to rubble and crawling with search and rescue teams continued to broadcast America's vulnerability. Most disturbing were pictures of the bisected cruise ship that languished half-submerged in Lower New York Bay. Surrounding the charred wreckage were hundreds of small boats that continued to circle, like fire ants milling around two disturbed nests.

As Sharon had stared at the scenes of devastation, thoughts of that horrible day flooded her mind. *My family is in there. It's been less than a week. Everything has changed.*

Lena's voice brought her back to the present. "Hey, are you okay?"

Like a dog shedding water, Sharon shook off her reverie. "Yes, the whole world seems to be falling apart. Look, Lena, I know everything is getting worse by the minute. The press is stoking the flames of anarchy, but to give me any chance of stopping future attacks, you've got to buy me a few days. Tell YKW that I've recorded the whole conversation with the subject on that pen you gave me. He told me that no more attacks are planned for at least the next week. First thing tomorrow, I'm going to copy the conversation on a flash drive and send it to you by courier. Tell YKW the worst thing would be to stage premature raids on a couple of bad apples when I have a plan to get the whole orchard."

Lena laughed. "Few bad apples?"

"What's so funny?" Sharon countered, slightly perturbed.

"You're amazing," Lena answered. "I'm sitting here in my suite listening to Mahler's Ninth and you hit me with the William Tell Overture."

Sharon smiled at the *Lone Ranger* analogy. "Glad I could lighten your load, *Kemo Sabe*. That's all for now. I'll call you tomorrow after my meeting with Dr. Ugly. I'm exhausted. Gonna hit the sack early."

As she pushed END on the cell phone, Lena sighed. *I had my day dodging bullets and shaking up the establishment, but I had help. With only her wits to guide her, Sharon has the guts to fly solo against a bunch of religious fanatics willing to die for their cause.*

Lena placed her cell on the bedside table, gazed at the suite's ornate ceiling and prayed. *Anne, if you have any clout left with the Big Guy up there, please ask Him to protect*

Sharon Richards from harm. Her family is dead, her cause is just and I'm in awe of her bravery.

DAY SEVEN

31

GRADUATE CENTER
CITY UNIVERSITY OF NEW YORK
MONDAY, 11:15 A.M.

DR. ABU MAZRA sat in his office, perplexed at his imam's cryptic orders and angry that a woman had the audacity to be fifteen minutes late for an appointment. Among the faculty at CUNY, Abu Mazra's misogyny was overt and legendary. "Women are only good for one thing, and they do that on their backs," the professor once told a stunned reporter during an interview, fully mindful of the outrage his statement would engender. But for his stellar credentials, he would have been banished from the university. As it was, among the various university faculties and student bodies he had become somewhat of an eccentric celebrity—a grumpy old lion to be admired from afar but seldom approached.

Born in Egypt, Muhammad Abu Mazra was the only child of a militant Muslim father and his cowed wife who never spoke her mind, if she spoke at all. Dedicating his life to the pursuit of knowledge, the young man excelled at various international universities, receiving paid scholarships and eventually earning his Ph.D. in Theoretical Physics at England's Oxford University. In his thirties, he immigrated to America and eventually became a naturalized citizen, all the while studying the tenets of radical Islam and the tactics of jihad under the guidance of his imam, Mustafa Shabbah.

Now in his late fifties, Abu Mazra had never married, opting instead for a voluminous library of pornography to satisfy his prurient needs.

A gentle knock on his door did nothing to assuage the professor's pent-up anger. "Enter," he barked loudly. Sharon Richards clicked on her pen recorder inside her blue kaftan kurti, opened the door and stepped into the professor's office. She had chosen to wear the same outfit from the day before. Ignoring hostile stares during her subway ride, she knew that Muslim resentment would be much less at a university than in other public venues. Sharon stuck her hand out. "Professor Muhammad Abu Mazra, I'm Malie. It's an honor…"

"You're late," he growled, ignoring her hand. "I'm only meeting with you as a favor to the imam, and you dare to be more than fifteen minutes late. Explain yourself."

Last night before going to bed, Sharon had studied this man through various sources on the internet. Her tardiness was deliberate, in order to gauge his anger and see him at his worst. "I apologize. I'm not yet used to New York's transportation subway system, plus I had to sign in…"

"That's no excuse," Abu Mazra interrupted again. "Get on with it. Who are you and why are you here?"

Sharon produced the same American passport she had used with the imam, handing it to the professor without comment. Like the imam, Abu Mazra compared the passport image to the woman standing before him. Seemingly satisfied with the likeness, he gave the document back to her. "Malak al-Insaf—

Angel of Justice. You want me to believe that you're the real Angel of Justice? If so..."

It was her turn to interrupt him. Sharon walked quickly around Abu Mazra's desk and loomed over him. She turned the shocked professor's chair to face her and planted both hands on his armrests. With a threatening sneer, she brought her face within inches of his. "I know. I'm dead. Killed in a drone attack, right? I've been through all of this with the imam and damned if I'm going to go through it all again with you. Just what did the imam tell you to do, Dr. High-and-Mighty?"

Abu Mazra bristled with indignity. No one at the university had ever dared to invade his space or mocked his name, let alone a woman in his office sanctuary. *But what if she is the real Angel of Justice?* he asked himself. *She has killed many and the imam trusts her.*

"To give you anything you need," he answered meekly, looking up at this dangerous woman with respect born of fear, "and include you in the preparations for Phase Three."

Sharon backed off, returning to the other side of his desk and continued with feigned arrogance, "Good answer, Pops. Now let's go someplace where we can talk, just the two of us."

A knock on the door preempted his response. Relieved at the interruption, Abu Mazra hastened to call out again. "Enter."

A thin man who looked to be in his late twenties walked through the entrance, stared at Sharon and came to a halt. He had never before seen a woman in the professor's office, let alone one this beautiful. "I-I'm s-sorry to interrupt..." he stammered and began to back out of the office.

The appearance of his protégé bolstered the professor's wounded psyche. Abu Mazra stood, came around his desk and gestured toward the woman. "Dr. Firouz Ahmed, meet Malak al-Insaf." Seeing the bewilderment on Ahmed's face, he added, "Yes, *that* Malak al-Insaf. As you can see, she is alive. With the imam's blessing, the Angel of Justice says she has come to help us."

As Ahmed came forward with an outstretched hand, the professor turned toward Sharon. "This is my assistant. He created the software to capture control of the airplanes that destroyed the cruise ship and two of America's most famous landmarks a week ago."

Knowing that she had now met the three terrorists most responsible for killing her family, Sharon willed herself to remain calm and stay in her role. Like a cobra waiting to strike, she stared into the young man's eyes and took his hand in hers. "I'm impressed, Dr. Ahmed. You must tell me exactly how you managed to achieve such spectacular results."

Mesmerized by her beauty yet wary of this woman's reputation, Ahmed hesitated to answer. Withdrawing his hand, he looked at the professor as if to say, "What now?"

Abu Mazra came to his rescue. "I suggest we have lunch at the Empire Room across the street. The restaurant will be crowded, but we should draw little notice from others."

To put the young man at ease, Sharon smiled before turning to the professor. "Fine with me, Pops. Lead the way."

Ahmed's mouth dropped open. *Pops? This woman has the gall to call the professor 'Pops'?* Seeing the look of astonishment on Ahmed's face, Sharon worked hard to stifle a laugh.

Over the span of the next two hours at the restaurant, Sharon Richards learned how the airplanes' auto-pilot controls were sabotaged with super-glue specially formulated to delay curing for two hours; how the planes had been "spoofed," or diverted toward their targets; the location of the cell's meeting place and workshop; the time of the next meeting; what they intended for Phase Three; and how many men were involved in this cell of terrorists calling themselves "al-Qaeda in America."

"Now it's my turn," Sharon said after listening without comment. "I congratulate both of you on your success, but with the three truck bombs, you had to use heavy and bulky ingredients like diesel fuel and ammonium nitrate. Devastating as those attacks were, they were primarily meant to be attention-getting statements against iconic landmarks. For your next phase, you're planning to hit a number of local shopping centers in order to strike fear throughout the country. You will be using primitive products purchased illegally in small quantities to avoid suspicion, some of which are unpredictable and dangerous to prepare. And to deliver each of these, you'll be depending on martyrs wearing suicide vests. Am I right?"

Both men nodded in agreement. The professor growled, "Our objective is to make every American afraid to leave his home. Do you have a better idea?"

Sharon leaned forward and stared at Abu Mazra with a look of certainty. "Yes," she said in a voice barely above a whisper.

"Stop wasting the lives of your faithful on suicide missions. That's 'old school.' The imam says you have unlimited funding. What if I can get you, say fifty bricks of military issue c-4?"

"Purchasing plastic explosives is illegal. How can you do this?" asked Ahmed, captivated by this brazen woman's zeal.

Sharon nodded soberly. "Over the last ten years, I have made contacts that have a good supply of military grade plastic explosives stolen from Army depots," Sharon lied, putting her hand on the young man's for emphasis. "I can get you pretty much anything if you have the money to pay for it."

Encouraged by their positive reaction, she decided to up the ante and reel them in. "Remember the London subway bombings in 2005—how devastating they were in such crowded quarters? I was one of the planners for that attack. Imagine the panic you can create by hiding one or two bricks of c-4, prepared with remote detonators and metal projectiles like ball bearings, nails or screws, and sealing them in brand-name kitchen appliance boxes. Have your soldiers leave these in high traffic areas of shopping centers like Walmart and Target stores throughout the country. Using burner phones, your men can set these bombs off at approximately the same time. If your goal is to paralyze this country's economy, can you think of a better way?"

Listening to this captivating woman's suggestion, the dour professor was uncharacteristically excited. "Can you deliver this much c-4 in three days...by our next meeting?"

Sharon hesitated. *The president promised to provide anything I need.* "I never offer what I can't produce, Pops,"

Sharon vowed confidently, praying that she could. "Now, here's what I propose…"

As the three left the restaurant, Dr. Abu Mazra was ebullient, praising Allah for sending him this insufferable but brilliant female soldier of jihad. Sharon Richards was deep in thought, wondering how she was going to sell the president on her hastily conceived plan.

Dr. Firouz Ahmed was simply in love.

The professor split off toward the CUNY graduate campus, leaving Firouz to walk beside Sharon to her rental car. The young man was nervously engaging in small talk, hoping to buy more time with this beautiful, dangerous woman. Sharon sensed his vulnerability and decided to strike.

"Why are you following me?" she asked, abruptly stopping on the busy sidewalk to look him in the eye.

"Because I-I…" he stuttered helplessly.

"You want to fuck me?"

Ahmed blushed and nodded, flustered by her boldness.

"Are you married? Have a live-in girlfriend?"

"N-no."

"Does anyone live with you?"

Again he shook his head.

"Where do you live? Give me your address," she continued. Pulling out a notepad and the pen recorder from under her kaftan kurti, she waited for his answer.

Ahmed complied nervously, wondering what would come out of her mouth next.

Sharon whispered in his ear, "My lover is dead and I am starved for sex. Do you think you can handle me? I am a tiger in bed."

Flushed with amorous expectations, Firouz Ahmed nodded eagerly. *Glory be to Allah, who has sent this beautiful angel to me, his lowly servant!*

"Then I will come to you on Wednesday night, ten o'clock," Sharon continued, smiling. *I've got him—hook, line and sinker.* "I'll be in disguise, in case your apartment building has security cameras. I will use the name 'Malie,' so you know it's me, okay?" She paused to make sure he understood.

He nodded.

"Now, do you have the time to show me the meeting place on Staten Island?"

"Anything for you," Firouz answered, giddy at the thought of spending another hour or two with this woman of his dreams.

"I'll drive. You give me directions," Sharon declared, lightly brushing her hand across the bulge in his pants. "I want to get to know you."

32

HAY-ADAMS HOTEL
9 P.M.

THROUGHOUT HER LIFE, Lena Mills had defied established conventions. She never used the words, "can't or "impossible," and had yet to meet anyone more stubborn than her...until now.

Plugging the flash drive into an Apple iPad, Sharon Richards had just finished playing the dialogue between her and the two terrorists. "Well, what do you think?" she asked Lena and her husband, Cal Carpenter. Both sat across from her at the dining room table.

Lena glanced at Cal, who looked like he was about to hack a hairball. He replied with a question that sounded more like a statement. "Let me get this straight. You want to deliver plastic explosives to terrorists, who will be using them to bomb shopping centers around the country."

"Yes, but..."

Cal interrupted, "Are you out of your friggin' mind?"

Sharon waited a few seconds, allowing him to chill before answering. "You're a former U.S. Marshal and I'm a retired FBI agent," she began with a calm voice. "We both know what I'm proposing is highly illegal. But, if you'll hear me out, I'll explain my plan in detail and the rationale behind it."

Lena glared daggers at her husband. "Let the lady present her case...without interruption." It was an order, not a request.

Sharon nodded to her new friend. "When we met with the president, she asked me to infiltrate the terrorist organization, find out who the leaders are, as well as their plans for future attacks. After listening to these recordings, we can all agree that I've been successful...right?"

Lena nodded. "You've exceeded the president's expectations."

"Do you remember what she asked me to do once I've gained the mastermind's confidence?"

"Yes," replied Lena. "Offer him assistance in planning future attacks." She glared at her husband as if to say, "So there!" Cal threw up his hands and left the room.

Sharon respected Cal but was glad to see him leave. She turned to Lena. "Let me lay it out for you, so you can lobby the president on my behalf. Assure her that I won't proceed until I get her green light, okay?"

Eager to hear the details, Lena nodded.

"I've seen the meeting place. It's an abandoned boatyard in a Staten Island swamp that stinks of decayed wood and fuel oil. To get there, you have to cross an ancient Dutch cemetery and walk a narrow path to avoid wading through inches of muck. The only structure with any kind of roof is a rusted out warehouse, which has to be their meeting place. I looked inside and there are new tables, chairs and a gas generator, which verifies it's a workshop, as Firouz Ahmed says.

"No one in their right mind, including the police, would go near this shit hole, especially at seven a.m. All-in-all, it seems an ideal place for these bastards to construct their bombs."

Lena held up a hand. "Once Liz hears your taped evidence, she'll want to send a team of U.S. Marshals to arrest the lot of them that morning."

"Which would be a big mistake, in my opinion," Sharon argued. "The mastermind, Dr. Muhammad Abu Mazra, is a Nobel Prize-winning physicist without even a traffic ticket to his name. It's the same with his assistant, Ahmed—no priors. Both are U.S. citizens, one naturalized and one by birth. The only evidence against them is on these recordings that most likely cannot be used against them in a court of law. There will be a trial that could last for years with no assurance of convictions. The country is traumatized and too angry to put up with that. We're at war, we know who the enemy is, and the American people want swift justice, not some bullshit show trial.

"My solution is effective, swift, but highly illegal. I can make the problem simply disappear, but I need you to talk the president into putting her assault team on standby in case something goes wrong, without knowing why. Convince her to let me do my thing."

Sharon paused. "I think you know what I'm talking about."

Lena studied this brash, confident woman sitting across from her. *God, to be twenty years younger*, she thought, *and have that fire in my belly.* She nodded soberly. "You'll need to camp out here until the meeting day. If you do leave, use the disguise I taught you. The last thing we want is for you to be recognized."

Sharon nodded in agreement.

"Now, let's go over the details," Lena said, retrieving a legal pad and pen. "I must have an iron-clad argument when I call on the president first thing tomorrow."

DAY EIGHT

33

THE WHITE HOUSE
OVAL OFFICE
TUESDAY, 10 A.M.

PRESIDENT ELIZABETH STANTON sat behind the Resolute Desk and stared at the flash drive like it was a cockroach she wanted to squash. She listened intently to the recorded interchanges twice before commenting. "Looks like we've got them dead to rights."

National Security Advisor Jack Gardner sat across the desk from her. "I'll instruct the U.S. Marshal Service to prepare for a raid early Thursday morning. We'll round up the entire cell..."

Lena Mills sat next to Gardner. "Madam President," she broke in. "I beg to differ."

Gardner's brow furrowed in anger at the interruption. "Who are you to interfere?"

It was the president's turn to interrupt her security advisor. "Jack, I want to hear what Ms. Mills has to say."

Gardner sat back and glowered at Lena. "Who's the woman on the tapes?"

The president signaled Lena to remain silent. "She's our best weapon against these terrorists and must remain anonymous."

"But I'm your National Security Advisor," Gardner protested. "Surely I have the clearance..."

"Jack, this is not a subject for debate. She stays anonymous, even to you."

Lena ignored the man and continued. "Liz, you charged her with infiltrating this terrorist cell and identifying the major players. She's done that, but you know as well as I do that none of what's on this flash drive will be admissible in a court of law. We're not dealing with international players. These are U.S. citizens and they have all the rights and privileges that go with that status. The coordinator is a Nobel Prize-winning physicist. If we charge in and arrest this bunch on Thursday, what will we accomplish, other than to create a media firestorm and temporarily foil their plans for more attacks?"

"Isn't that enough?" broke in Gardner.

"No, it isn't," answered Stanton. "I agree with Lena and I want to hear her out—uninterrupted." Her look of warning said, *Shut up or get out!*

"The woman has won their confidence, and if you recall, you also asked her to offer assistance in future attacks," Lena continued, ignoring the cold stare from Gardner. "She's stuck her neck out and promised to deliver the bricks of c-4 and materials necessary to build remote detonators to this meeting on Thursday. I say we let her do just that."

Jack Gardner stood and exploded, "This is outrageous! We don't give weapons to terrorists."

Lena looked at Gardner and countered, "Are you kidding? Do 'Iran-Contra' and 'Fast and Furious' mean anything to you?"

Meanwhile, Stanton pushed a button on her intercom and calmly asked, "Madelyn, please get me a roll of Duct tape. There's a hot air leak in here."

Gardner flushed beet red and stormed toward the Oval Office entrance. "Wait!" snapped President Stanton. The man stopped and turned toward her with a look of hatred.

"Okay Jack, I apologize for the cheap shot. I've given you a chance to continue from the previous administration as my National Security Advisor, but after two months it's obvious we don't agree on anything. Therefore, I will expect your resignation by tomorrow noon, earliest."

Gardner's mouth dropped open in surprise.

"And if any part of this meeting ends up in the press," Stanton added, "I'll know the leak came from you. Make no mistake, Jack. I'll make it my top priority to make your life so miserable you'll wish you were never born. Do you understand?"

With his shoulders slumped in defeat, Gardner turned and walked out of the Oval Office muttering profanity under his breath.

The president turned to Lena. "I'm sorry. That man has been a thorn in my side since I took the oath of office. I thought I needed his advice during the transition, but I was wrong. He shouldn't have been at this meeting."

Lena nodded in agreement.

"Now," Stanton continued, "tell me about Sharon's plan—every last detail."

34

FBI REGIONAL FIELD OFFICE
PHILADELPHIA, PENNSYLVANIA
TUESDAY, NOON

"FBI, LAMBERT SPEAKING."

"Will, Sharon." At the sound of her voice, Special Agent Will Lambert sat forward in his seat.

"Where have you been? What…?"

"I can't explain anything over the phone," she interrupted, "but as I said before, you're the only one I can trust. So hear me out and don't ask questions, okay?"

"Fire away," Lambert replied. He was used to his former second-in-charge being abrupt.

"A woman named Lena Mills is coming to meet with you. Yes, she's *that* Lena Mills."

"I remember her," he acknowledged, thinking, *What's with all the intrigue?*

"I need you to provide her with anything she asks for, including some things I remember that you still have in the cold file evidence locker. I know all this sounds crazy and I can't talk about it, even over this encrypted line. Everything must remain confidential between you, me and Ms. Mills. I'm asking you to cooperate under the authority of the President of the United States. Understand? It's that confidential."

Lambert was intrigued. Something big was going on and Sharon was right in the middle of it. "Does this have anything to do with...?"

"No questions, Will," Sharon interrupted again. "Everything will be made clear in a few days...and yes, it's a matter of national security."

The lady reads my mind, thought Lambert, silenced by the enormity of her words.

"And Will, I have one more favor to ask of you. Let me borrow Hamp for a few days, strictly off the reservation. Have him prepare to return with Lena and the things she requests." Sharon paused, thinking, *I'd love to be a fly in the corner of that limo.*

"Of course, Sharon. Anything else?"

"Wish us luck, Will. We're gonna need it."

With that, Lambert was left with a dial tone. Bewildered, he replaced the receiver on its console and punched Agent Ron Hampton's intercom number. "Hamp, go home and pack," he ordered. "You're about to go on the most bizarre field trip of your life."

35

HAY-ADAMS HOTEL
6 P.M.

LENA MILLS and Agent Ron Hampton entered the Lafayette Suite chattering like two ground squirrels bickering over a juicy nut. "You're one crazy lady," Hampton complained, waving his arms. "Three hours with you and I'm ready for the Funny Farm. My mama is a stubborn old broad, but she's not half as bad as you."

"Obviously, your mama didn't discipline you when you were little," countered Lena, who seemed to be enjoying their verbal jousting. "Didn't she teach you to respect your elders?"

Frustrated, Hampton was turning as red as his African-American complexion would allow. "Respect? How can I respect someone who's so...wrong?"

Sharon looked at Cal, who was trying to stifle a chuckle. The two had spent most of the day talking about their careers and beliefs. Like two long-lost relatives, both realized they had much in common. Sharon rose from the living room sofa and wedged herself between the two combatants. "Hey, you two," she chided. "Do I need to get out the boxing gloves?"

Lena was the first to back down. Laughing, she put an arm around Hampton's shoulder and looked at her husband. "I love this guy. He reminds me of a young Claude—feisty and obstinate."

Indignant, Hampton pulled away from her embrace. "Who you callin' a clod?"

Cal rose and approached the young man with an outstretched hand. "Not clod...Claude," he corrected, shaking Ron's hand. "She means Claude Masters, her life-long friend. It's a compliment. He's in a room down the hall and more obstinate than Lena if you can believe it. I'm Lena's husband, Cal Carpenter. Now, what's all the fuss about?"

Lena grinned. "Nothing important. We're both jazz buffs. I think Ella Fitzgerald was the greatest female jazz singer of all time, and he likes Diana Krall. We've been yanking each other's chains all the way from Philly. I haven't had this much fun arguing since Claude and I used to go at each other many years ago."

Hampton would not give up. "I can't believe I'm debating this relic." Turning to Sharon, he added, "Tell Miz M I'm right, Mama Dough."

Sharon looked confused. "Who's Diana Krall?"

Ron blanched a lighter shade of pale. His mouth dropped open in disbelief.

"Who're you calling a relic?" snapped Lena. "I'll take you over my knee and..."

"What's this about Mama Dough?" interrupted Cal.

Everyone stopped yelling and focused on Hampton. Lena and Cal looked at him quizzically, while Sharon stared daggers at her former FBI colleague, thinking, *How much does Ron know about Duncan's inheritance?*

Hampton knew that look. He was on thin ice with his former boss and deflected the issue. "Sharon's pet name for her husband was Donut, as in *Dunkin Donuts*. I called him Papa Dough, and outside the office, Sharon was Mama Dough." He looked at Sharon for her approval.

Lena and Cal seemed to accept the explanation. Sharon breathed a sigh of relief and changed the subject. "Look, we're here to do something very serious. Let's get on with it. Hamp, what do you know about your assignment? Do you know why you're here?"

"The boss said this would be a 'bizarre field trip,' and it's a matter of national security. Why are there fifty bricks of c-4 in the limousine trunk?"

Obviously uninformed, Cal glared at Lena with worry. "C-4? What the hell are you doing with c-4?"

Lena looked at her husband, then at Ron. "We're sorry for all the secrecy. Other than the president, her National Security Advisor and the people in this room, no one knows what Sharon and I are about to tell you, and it has to stay that way."

Looking at Cal, Sharon joined in. "To answer your question, at seven a.m. on Thursday we're going to deliver the c-4 and the materials to make remote detonators to a home-grown terrorist cell."

"With strings attached, of course," Lena added, pausing to enjoy Sharon's flair for the dramatic. "We've identified the group of jihadists responsible for all the bombings these past few days, and the president has given us the green light to destroy the lot of them."

Before elaborating, the women let this answer sink in. Both men's jaws dropped. It was Sharon's turn to explain. "We've got one day to shop for the remote detonator materials and burner phones, as well as rehearse this mission. It has to be coordinated perfectly. Each of us will be playing a vital role in the mission's success..."

"Count me out," Cal interrupted, disgusted. Heading for the suite's bedroom, he added, "What you're talking about has to be highly illegal. Not only won't I participate, I don't want to hear any more."

Perturbed, Lena followed her husband and caught him before he slammed the bedroom door. "You think we're crazy. I get that. But we're acting on behalf of the president. I only ask three things of you. Trust us, keep all this to yourself and don't interfere."

Cal took her in his arms. Tears were forming in his eyes. "We've got a great life, Lena. I don't want to lose what we have."

"That's why I'm—we're—doing this, darling," she answered, melting in his arms. "I don't want to lose it either, and if we do nothing, we're about to lose everything by default. Sharon is in a unique position. The leaders of this cell trust her. Her plan is simple and the probability of success is high. Just remember, the president has signed off on this. That's all you need to know." She backed away and looked into his eyes.

Cal sighed in resignation and entered the bedroom. "Do what you're gonna do. I'm too old for this shit," he mumbled, closing the door.

Sharon welcomed Lena back into the fold and picked up a legal pad and pencil, gesturing toward the dining room table. "Tomorrow we go shopping." When Lena and Ron were seated, the former FBI agent began drawing a strategic timeline. "We've only got one crack at this, so we must be sure of each step, yet flexible. Now let's look at all the things that could possibly go wrong..."

DAY NINE

36

BROOKLYN, NEW YORK
WEDNESDAY, 1 P.M.

IMAM MUSTAFA SHABBAH was in his office when his cell phone rang. Only two people had the phone's pre-programmed number—Professor Muhammad Abu Mazra and Malak al-Insaf, the Angel of Justice. The imam was expecting this call.

"Uncle Baba, this is Malie."

"Do you have everything?" They had agreed to avoid using specific descriptions in case the encryption was compromised.

"Yes, fifty, as agreed upon. I will speak slowly, so you can take notes. Are you ready?"

"Yes, my dear. Very slowly please."

Sharon waited a few seconds before reading from her written script. "Tomorrow morning at six-thirty I will arrive at the back door of your office. Leave it unlocked. I will knock two times, pause, then two more times to let you know it's me. After you give me the agreed sum in cash, I will call my driver to deliver the load to the cemetery lot, where your men will be waiting for him."

She paused again. "Let me know when you're ready for me to continue."

A few seconds passed. "Yes. Go ahead."

"The driver is a young black man who works for my source. He doesn't know what's in the boxes and will also use my nickname "Malie" to identify himself. Everything is packaged in seven boxes, none of them weighing more than twenty pounds. Once your men unload the truck, the driver will leave. Have your men carry the boxes on the short path to your meeting place. Do you have all of this? If so, please repeat it to me."

"Give me a few more seconds," the imam replied, scribbling notes on a pad of paper. "Okay, I have everything. But what will happen then?"

"Tell your leader that I will come to the meeting place and show the team how to assemble the items as well as how to distribute them for maximum effect. Now, repeat everything that I have told you."

The imam slowly read his notes back to Sharon.

"Good. Now remember, tomorrow morning, six-thirty, back door."

"I will be waiting for you."

37

THE WHITE HOUSE
SITUATION ROOM
5 P.M.

PRESIDENT ELIZABETH STANTON paced the floor like a caged lioness. No one dared to interrupt the president when she was in a mood to kill. The national media was constantly demanding updates. Congressional calls for presidential impeachment were becoming more strident with each passing hour.

Despite the imposition of martial law and curfews in the nation's largest cities, protests continued unabated. The economy was at a standstill. Most Americans remained sequestered in their homes, fearing the protesters more than the next terrorist attack. Around the world, equity markets continued their downward spiral. Rioting was even worse in countries that were declaring insolvency. Illegal aliens, many of whom were potential terrorists, were streaming across the southern border, virtually unchallenged by an overwhelmed border patrol and local law enforcement. In short, the United States of America was on the brink of disaster.

Four key members of the president's inner circle, Press Secretary Jackie Roman, Secretary of Homeland Security

Margo Smith, Vice President Eldon Bennett and Chairman of the Joint Chiefs of Staff General Mike Jablonsky, sat waiting for her to speak. Noticeably absent was the National Security Advisor.

Stanton stopped pacing and focused her attention on Secretary Smith. "Margo, yesterday I had to dismiss Jack Gardner. The reason should be obvious, so I need not go into details. Until further notice, you will be liaising with his assistant, Kate Irminger. She and I also have our differences, but at least, Kate is willing to follow orders."

Secretary Smith nodded soberly without comment.

The president directed her gaze toward Jablonsky. "General, we all know what's happening here on the homefront. Bring me up to date on the Middle East."

Never at a loss for words, Jablonsky preferred profanity over diplomacy. The president often chastised the bombastic five-star general in public while secretly appreciating his blunt assessments. "Madam President, as you know, Israel has been kicking ass in the region for decades. The previous administration has hung the Jewish state out to dry, emboldening her hostile neighbors.

"Thanks to the campaign of bombing by us and our allies, the Islamic State, or ISIL, and other al-Qaeda offshoots have been halted in the acquisition of new territory, but continue their social media recruiting as well as beheadings on YouTube.

"Now that Iran has nukes and the ability to deliver them long distances, it's a new ballgame. With America's domestic attacks diverting our attention away from international matters, Iran promises to strike Israel with nuclear missiles at any time. The Israeli Ambassador contacted me yesterday. He has been asking Secretary of State Clanton for a one-on-one meeting between you and the President of Israel for over a week, even if it's on the phone. But the ambassador hasn't received a response, and he thinks we have abandoned his country. What should I tell him?"

Stanton could feel her blood pressure spike. "This is news to me," she growled, punching a button on the intercom. "Madelyn, tell Dan Clanton I want him to drop whatever he's doing and meet me at the Oval Office in one hour. Also, please ask the Ambassador of Israel to attend. Offer him my apologies for not meeting with his president, and tell him that I had no knowledge of the request for an audience. Tell him he'll have a front-row seat when I fire my Secretary of State, but do not relate this to Clanton. Do you have all that? Good."

She turned her attention back to Jablonsky. "Mike, raise our national threat level to DEFCON 2 and inform the media immediately. Later today, I will call the President of Iran and remind him that if his country releases one ballistic missile toward the State of Israel, we will cripple his country's defense infrastructure and unleash the full weight of our arsenal on his country's nuclear facilities."

Everyone in the room sat at attention, amazed at the president's reiteration of her bold and pernicious threat. General Mike Jablonsky beamed with pride. *This woman has the balls of a gladiator.*

Addressing the four people she could count on to follow her orders without complaint, President Stanton added, "Now, back to our problem here at home. The American people are tired of being kicked around by a few home-grown radicals. The polls show that over ninety percent of Americans are demanding that we become proactive instead of reactive.

"Margo, notify the media that, effective immediately, I am canceling my order for martial law and lifting all curfews throughout the country. They were ineffective, knee-jerk reactions to the bombings, as well as a sign of weakness to the rest of the world.

"Alert the fifty governors that I expect them to send all available National Guard troops to the southern border and repel, by force if necessary, anyone crossing it. I will call the presidents of Mexico and the Central American countries that have taken advantage of our porous borders and tell them we're cutting off all aid immediately until they prove they have stopped the exodus of their citizens to our country. How they do it is their problem. We're going to lock down this country's borders like a virgin's corset.

"This next week will decide whether the greatest nation on earth can restore its preeminence in the world or become another failed attempt at democracy relegated to the trash heap of history. I'll be damned if it's going to be the latter."

With that, she punched the intercom again. "Madelyn, I'm going to the Oval Office. Please connect me to the President of Israel so I can apologize and update him on what we're doing."

Stanton marched out of the room, leaving her stunned associates to argue the state of their president's mental condition.

38

QUEENS, NEW YORK
10 P.M.

DRESSED IN HER DISGUISE, Sharon Richards knocked softly on the door of Firouz Ahmed's apartment. He waited until she said the password before opening the door and greeting her with a nervous hug. A slight odor of sandalwood incense irritated her sinuses. *God, I hope I don't lapse into a sneezing fit,* she prayed. Stifling the urge, Sharon smiled and stripped out of her disguise, signaling the intention to shed her undergarments as well.

Muted sounds of Indian string music played in the background. "Is that a sitar?" she asked, pointing to his small entertainment center. "Ravi Shankar?" she added.

Ahmed was impressed and temporarily ignored his sexual ardor. "Yes. He was popular well before either of us was born, but no one has ever played the sitar like the great Ravi. I listen to him often for inspiration. Did you know that his daughter is a famous American composer and singer, Nora Jones?"

"Yes, she is a favorite of mine," Sharon lied, unaware of the fact.

"May I get you a glass of wine, or something stronger?" he asked.

She wagged her finger at him provocatively. "Some Muslim you are, Firouz Ahmed. I do not drink alcohol and neither should you."

"The same could be said of sex outside of marriage," he challenged her, immediately regretting his blunder.

Sharon gauged his forlorn expression and decided to initiate her advance. Locking his front door, she answered, "You know what I came for." Kicking off her shoes, she seductively paraded around him, clothed only in a bra and panties. "Like what you see?"

Firouz gulped. "Oh, yes."

"Then let me see how big that bulge of yours really is. I've been playing with it inside your pants all the way to the meeting place and back this afternoon." She unhooked his belt buckle and smiled, her face within inches of his. "I'll show you mine if you'll show me yours."

Shedding his clothes in record time, Firouz Ahmed stood before her, naked and erect. As he stepped forward, Sharon held up one hand and gripped his throbbing member with the other. *He must be ten inches.*

"Whoa, stud! Slow down. Let me set the ground rules. I like to dominate, and that means you lie on the bed and I strap your hands and feet to the posts. Understand? Are you okay with that?"

In his present state, Firouz was only worried about one thing—premature ejaculation. "Yes, anything you want," he rasped, his mouth suddenly dry. Allowing her to lead him to his queen-sized bed, he lay on his back and waited for his lover to shed her undergarments, thinking, *I don't know how long I can last.*

Sharon was disgusted but suppressed her emotions. "Don't move," she ordered, pulling four sturdy black leather straps from her bag. "First, I tie you down, then I take off the rest of my clothes." She grinned seductively. "You're in for the ride of your life."

Sharon climbed on his chest, wound and hooked the leather straps around his wrists and secured each to a bedpost. She reversed herself on his body and did the same to his ankles, giving him a generous look at her barely covered backside. Before climbing off his torso, she gave his enormous erection a short stroke, causing him to groan in ecstasy.

Satisfied that he was securely tethered, she slowly unhooked her bra and let it drop to the floor, smiling wickedly. "How about now?"

"You're the most beautiful woman I've ever seen, praise be to Allah!" he exclaimed. "I am about to explode."

Sharon grabbed her bag and pulled out a small roll of Duct tape. "Hold that thought, lover. There's one more thing."

Firouz groaned. This was excruciating, worse than the prick teasing his girlfriend used to give him during his senior year of high school.

Ripping off a generous length of the silver-colored adhesive, she climbed on his chest again, smashing the tape across his mouth and both sides of his jaw line. "We don't want to bother the neighbors when you scream, right?" Sharon whispered in his ear. Muffled sounds of protest told her that he was beginning to worry.

Inching up another foot, she reversed herself, kneeled on both sides of his head and squeezed her knees. "Does this hurt?" she asked, squeezing harder. Ignoring his muffled cry of pain, she added, "Not nearly as much as this will."

Sharon pulled out a large hypodermic syringe from her bag and flashed it in front of his eyes that were now bulging with terror. "You see, I'm not who you think I am, you son-of-a-bitch," she stated calmly. "My name is Sharon Richards, and I was on that cruise ship you destroyed."

Trembling with fear, Firouz Ahmed knew he was about to die. His lower body thrashed from side to side as he tried in vain to scream. Sharon was pleased to see that his neck muscles were taut, causing the veins to swell.

Squeezing her thigh muscles with all her might, she locked down his head and pulled back the plunger, filling the syringe with forty cubic centimeters of air. "My husband and two sons were on that ship," she growled. "I lived. They died. YOU...KILLED...MY...FAMILY!"

Sharon's eyes were cold as ice as she inserted the needle into Ahmed's jugular vein and pushed the plunger all the way home. "Now it's your turn."

Like a lion gazing at a crippled gazelle, she looked into the eyes of her kill. For a few seconds, a curious sense of sexual release made her shudder. Loosening her grip on Ahmed's head, Sharon pulled out the needle and backed off his now limp body. The combination of expelled urine, feces and the room's incense revolted her, but she waited a few minutes for the pulmonary embolism to take full effect.

Ripping the tape from his face, Sharon checked for a pulse on her victim's neck and wrist. Feeling none, she wet her hand with a splash of water from the kitchen sink and held it close to her victim's nose to detect any sign of breathing.

Firouz Ahmed was dead.

Sharon unhooked the leather straps and let Ahmed's limbs fall by his side. Pulling a pair of cotton gloves from her bag, she wiped down the bedposts, kitchen sink lever, doorknob and his belt buckle. *Did I miss anything?* She racked her brain to recall her long-ago FBI forensic training and all the *CSI* programs she had watched on television. What else could possibly lead investigators to implicate her in this mysterious death? The answer was obvious.

She donned the gloves and looked under the sink for cleaning supplies. Finding a squeegee mop in a nearby closet, Sharon put her shoes on and, using a wood cleaner, she wiped all the areas where she had walked with her bare feet. Then she sprayed a wet rag with a dollop of liquid Dove soap and wiped away any of her DNA from Ahmed's chest, legs, head, neck and penis. Sharon rinsed the same areas with another wet rag without soap.

The needle prick on Ahmed's neck was almost invisible. There was nothing she could do to make it disappear completely, but she knew that the lethal injection of air would leave no chemical evidence of foul play.

Satisfied that she had done the best job possible sanitizing the apartment and her victim, she dressed again in costume, packed everything she had brought into her bag, triple-checked the room for anything she may have missed, peeked both ways for anyone in the hallway, closed the door and walked to her car.

Sharon scanned the apartment parking lot and was relieved to see that she was alone. She climbed in the driver seat and checked her watch—10:47. Consumed with worry, everything she had been through, everything she had done since the airplane crashed into the cruise ship, finally hit home.

Right or wrong, tonight I've taken a path that cannot be retracted. I'm a murderer, just like the men who killed my family and thousands of innocent human beings. I have no family and few friends I can trust. God, what do I have to live for except revenge?

There were no answers, only a feeling of guilt, much worse than the time she had lost her virginity to Duncan in the back seat of his car during their senior year of high school.

For the first time since that fateful afternoon of terror eight days ago, she broke down and cried. A half-hour and a box of Kleenex later, she regained enough control to drive to her Manhattan apartment, where Ron Hampton was waiting outside the door.

"Where you been, boss?" he asked. "You didn't leave me a key." Seeing Sharon's red eyes, he immediately regretted the question and gave her a hug. "Sorry. All this finally got to you, huh?"

She opened the door and entered her apartment, motioned for Ron to sit at the kitchen table and joined him. Sharon blew her nose on another wad of Kleenex. "Yeah, but this is the first time I've ever killed someone face-to-face, so cut me some slack, okay?"

"Whoa! I thought what happened to Duncan and the kids finally hit home, and you're telling me that you offed somebody today? Fill me in."

"The guy who invented the program to hijack the airplanes. Long story short, I killed him at his apartment tonight and covered my tracks to make it look like natural causes. At least, I think I did," she added. "He was responsible for thousands of deaths, including my family, and deserved to rot in Hell. I should feel good about it, but I don't."

Hampton held both of her arms and stared into her eyes with sympathy. "Look at it this way, Sharon. He was a dead man walking, whether you did the deed today or I did it tomorrow morning. I know what you're feeling. I felt the same way after my first field kill. You never grow immune to it, but the guilt diminishes in time. The bleeding hearts call it lack of humanity." He stood back and waved a hand in the air. "Screw 'em. Like the hit man I killed for Papa Dough, these jihadists are murdering insects and I'm the *Orkin Man*."

Sharon forced a smile and asked, "Where were you the last two days?"

"Making sure everything is ready for tomorrow," he answered, glad that her mind was back on track. "I spent most of today at our Staten Island storage unit, packing all seven boxes exactly alike—four with inactive ten packs of c-4 bricks and shrapnel, two containing twenty burner phones, detonators and wiring..." He pulled out his iPhone, "and one with an active IED containing shrapnel and the remaining ten c-4 bricks wired in tandem. They're ready to blow when I punch this. He pointed to SEND."

Sharon had a question, but let Hamp continue. "Then I drove upstate and found a local park to practice my skills at flying our Dragonfly X-6 drone and operating the optical zoom. I drew a small crowd but told them I was just a hobbyist enjoying the day. As long as the weather holds tomorrow morning, everything should go as planned."

"What happens if someone like a salesman or a robo-marketer dials the same number and activates the IED?" she asked.

"I took care of that, too. I went to see an FBI tech bud of mine in D.C. and he added 'restricted contact' to the receiver, so it will only accept the call from my phone." He rose from his seat and danced a modified soft-shoe, hoping to cheer her up. "Ol' Hamp ain't gonna do no *Dr. Strangelove*, no ma'am!"

Sharon smiled, feeling somewhat better. "Duncan said you're the most creative son-of-a-bitch he ever met."

"And do you know what he said about you?"

She shook her head.

"That he loved you more than life itself and didn't deserve you."

Sharon's eyes welled up again as if she had been verbally sucker-punched. "Thanks for that, Hamp. I've worked with you for over four years. You seem to know everything about me, but other than your age of thirty-two and that you're single, I know very little about you."

"What do you want to know?"

"What are your goals, career and otherwise? Do you have—what's the term?—a significant other?"

Ron sat back down. "Well, I like the career path I'm on with the FBI, and I especially liked working with Will and you—until you resigned, that is. I know I could make a lot more money working for a private company, but the risk and reward of catching bad guys fascinate me."

He hesitated. "As for my love life, there is one lady who floats my boat. I met her at a friend's wedding about six months ago. Her name is Sharon, like yours, and she's an elementary teacher at the Montessori School in Gladwyne, where the rich folks live. I haven't popped any questions to her, but I can see us 'together forever,' as the saying goes."

Sharon rose from her seat. *This guy's the real deal.* "I'm happy for you, Hamp." She pointed to the second bedroom. "Now let's get some shut-eye. We've got a long day ahead of us."

Closing the door to her room, she set the alarm to four a.m. and cried herself to sleep.

DAY TEN

39

STATEN ISLAND, NEW YORK
THURSDAY, 6:30 A.M.

DAWN HAD BARELY BROKEN over a clear sky at the ancient Dutch cemetery when the soldiers of al-Qaeda in America began arriving. The brisk morning air did little to dampen the stench of the swamp, old fuel oil and decayed wood, but most of the men had become used to the dankness. Besides, no one dared to test the professor's volatile temper. At best, any complaints would have fallen on deaf ears.

Dr. Abu Mazra acknowledged each man with a grunt and handshake. In a rare gesture of consideration, the professor had brought twenty-five Styrofoam cups of hot coffee to the meeting and left them in the building some one-hundred yards from the parking area. "Go get a cup and return here by seven," he ordered. "A shipment is supposed to arrive by truck. I'll need a few of you to carry boxes to the building. We have a long morning ahead of us."

The professor was annoyed. *Where is Firouz?* Two cell phone calls to his brilliant assistant had gone unanswered. *He was supposed to be here at six. This is not at all like him.*

Abu Mazra's irritation was short-lived, however. Ahmed's cerebral skills wouldn't be needed for this next phase. Today he would be just another set of hands assembling remote-controlled bombs.

The professor counted heads. Except for Ahmed, all of his soldiers were present by six forty-five. He paced back and forth like a caged lion, knowing there was nothing he could do now but wait. He hated that the mission was dependent on the brash young woman's competence, but the imam had expressed confidence in her.

Insha'Allah, he prayed silently. *Insha'Allah.*

40

BROOKLYN, NEW YORK
6:30 A.M.

DRESSED IN HER black kaftan kurti and matching cap, Sharon Richards surveyed the mosque parking lot. Aside from her car, it was empty. No worshippers were in sight, nor were any expected at this hour. She parked in a spot next to the back door.

Lightly knocking twice as planned, she turned the knob and entered the imam's sanctuary. Shabbah greeted her with a hug. "You're very punctual." Pointing to two chairs across from one another, he added, "We have time. Let us talk for a minute. What is in the bag?"

"Tools and copies of instructions for making the remote-controlled IEDs," she replied, pulling out a sheet of paper and giving it to the imam. "Where are your guards?"

Shabbah perused the page with casual interest. "They are with Dr. Abu Mazra, waiting for you."

Sharon smiled. *The imam is alone and making it easier for me. He must trust me completely.* "I have made arrangements to deliver the c-4 that I promised you, Uncle Baba. I trust you will be pleased with my service as well. Upon leaving here, I will go to the meeting place and oversee the preparation of these 'instruments of retribution.'

"Once they are assembled, the professor has a list of destinations throughout the country for your followers to deliver and simultaneously execute Phase Three. They will kill many infidels without harming themselves, so they can return to fight again. If Americans feel they cannot trust the safety of shopping centers, they will stay home and cower in fear, knowing they are subject to Allah's wrath no matter where they go."

Shabbah smiled benevolently. "You truly have been a timely gift from the Almighty, my dear. Your plan is brilliant in its simplicity and ease of execution. The price you ask seems high, but if we achieve the results as you suggest, your price should be no object."

With that, the imam rose from his seat and spun the dial to his large wall safe. "I have the money you asked for," he said, opening the lock.

Sharon was on him in two seconds, racing from her seat to wrap her arms around his neck and pull him to the floor. The swiftness of the attack made the imam grunt in surprise but gave her a couple of seconds to produce the roll of Duct tape from the carrying bag and plaster his mouth with a large strip, stifling his scream.

At his age, the imam was no match for the younger and skilled former FBI agent, who held his torso and arms down with her legs while her hands pulled from the bag a syringe filled with a light yellow liquid. Removing the needle cover, she plunged it into his neck.

Shabbah's legs kicked out in panic, but his leather-soled shoes failed to hit anything except the wood laminate floor, causing a muted tapping sound. Sharon looked down at the imam and smiled, knowing the more he resisted, the faster the drug would work. She looked at her wristwatch—6:49. With the imam under control, she bent over to whisper in his ear. "I am not your precious Malie. I am your worst nightmare. Soon you're going to feel disoriented and unable to talk or move. Then you and I are going to take a little trip."

Sharon took two small iPhones from under her tunic and texted two burn notes. One was to Dr. Abu Mazra on the phone given to her by the imam. *Delivery on the way. Blue F-150. I'll be there less than an hour.*

She typed the other message on Lena's phone—a one-word message to Ron Hampton. *Proceed.*

41

LA TOURETTE PARK
STATEN ISLAND
6:50 A.M.

HAMPTON ACKNOWLEDGED Sharon's message with "OK," put his iPhone on the console of the rented pickup truck and drove out of the park onto the Pearl Harbor Memorial Highway. He had been awake since four a.m., first driving to the storage unit, then loading all seven boxes onto the truck bed. He hid the disassembled Dragonfly mini-helicopter and its aerial video platform under a blanket in back of the truck's super cab. If Sharon had been successful convincing the terrorists of his role as an ignorant delivery man, no one would search the cab. But if they did, he would tell them the drone was for another customer. At any rate, he was to call Sharon if any problems arose.

Yesterday Hampton had carefully checked his bomb's wiring, tandem connections and the modified cell phone three times before sealing the wrapped package and surrounding shrapnel inside one of the boxes. There would be only one chance at success and no way to test the device in advance.

A couple of miles down the highway he veered onto an access road and followed it about a quarter mile to the cemetery entrance. Twenty-two scruffy-looking men were waiting. Three of the young men carried what looked like Uzi pistols and surrounded an older man. *Must be Abu Mazra.*

Throwing the truck into PARK, Hampton opened his door and decided to lighten the tense atmosphere. "Whew! Sure do stink around here. I'm Hamp. Malie sent me. Who's the boss?"

Ron pointed to the cargo bed. Abu Mazra stepped forward and, without a word, signaled his men to unload the boxes. It took less than a minute. "Okay, I get it," Hampton added. "No small talk, nuthin' to sign. Have a nice life. I'm outta here."

The men turned toward the cemetery. Hampton's pulse was racing, yet he forced himself to stroll calmly to the truck, wondering, *Can it be this easy?*

Ron got in and drove off, breathing a sigh of relief. *Now comes the fun part.*

About two hundred yards, just past a curve in the access road, Hampton stopped, got out of the truck and quickly assembled the helicopter drone. Placing it on the ground, he booted up the handheld controller and sent the silent drone about five hundred feet into the air. Pointing the camera toward his targets and zooming the lens, he observed seven men carrying the boxes toward the building. The rest were following single-file across the narrow walkway. In another minute, all were inside.

Timing was essential. Hampton quickly recalled the drone, putting it and the controller into the back bed of the truck, fully assembled. He drove off, pulling the iPhone from his front pocket. Taking a deep breath, Ron poised his finger over SEND. *This is for you, Papa Dough.*

Two agonizing seconds went by before Hampton felt the concussion. His rear view mirror lit up like a sunburst. The explosion was deafening. *No one could live through that.* Punching Sharon's speed dial number, he texted "Done."

Ecstatic that he had completed his assignment without a hitch, Hampton drove more than five miles before he heard sirens. A number of fire trucks and ambulances passed him, racing the other way toward the scene of destruction.

The next stop was a funeral home in Brooklyn, where Sharon Richards and Lena Mills would be waiting. On the way, his thoughts turned to his former boss. Her mission was much more difficult and subject to chance. She was tough, but would her emotions come into play? Under the same circumstances, would his? Damn right they would!

Keep your head, Mama Dough, he prayed, *keep your head.*

42

THE BROOKLYN MOSQUE
7 A.M.

SHARON RICHARDS looked down at Imam Mustafa Shabbah. His eyes had rolled back and his body had grown limp. Her iPhone vibrated. It was Hamp's one-word message. Pleased with the news, she put the phone back in her pocket and eased off the imam's chest and arms. Checking his neck, she felt for a pulse. It was strong.

Seeing that her victim offered no resistance, Sharon opened a folded canvas bag from the larger one she had brought with her and cleaned out the imam's safe. There was no time to count the stacks of hundred-dollar bills or read the two small notebooks that were inside. She just stuffed them into the bag.

Following Lena's order, she rifled through the imam's personal file cabinet and quickly removed a file marked "Medical Reports" and added it to the bag. Then, as she had the previous night, Sharon put on white cotton gloves, closed the safe and wiped down all the surfaces she had touched. Opening the back door, she surveyed the parking lot in both directions. Like before, no one was in sight.

Throwing the bag straps over her head, she leveraged the imam to his feet and dragged his limp body to her car. Using two medium-sized pillows, she wedged his body upright in the front seat. *Maybe it's my adrenaline kicking in, but for such a big man he seems easier to maneuver than I had anticipated.*

Returning to the back entrance, Sharon quickly wiped down the handles on both sides, then locked and closed the door, hoping she had bought enough time to escape before anyone showed up for work or prayers. Before leaving, she keyed Hamp's speed dial on Lena's iPhone again and texted, "On my way with the package."

Driving to her destination would take a little more than thirty minutes. Silent until now, Sharon began to talk as she started the car. "I know you can understand me. You're confused and scared. Your whole team of terrorists—Dr. Abu Mazra, Firouz Ahmed and more than twenty soldiers of your al-Qaeda in America, are dead.

"I am not Malie, your Angel of Justice. My name is Sharon Richards. I was with my family on board that cruise ship you destroyed ten days ago." Tears of outrage formed in her eyes. Her hands began to shake with rage. *Don't lose it now. Stay strong.*

Sharon shook off her emotions and glanced at the imam. Unable to move, the look of fear in his eyes told her that he understood her every word. "I survived, but my husband and two sons died in the explosion. My family burned to death. Today you will die the same way."

The imam moaned helplessly, trying in vain to speak. "Go ahead, asshole," Sharon continued, "fight it. The shot I gave you was a tranquilizer called ketamine. In medical terms, it's called a dissociative anesthetic. That means you know what's

216

happening, but you can't respond physically. Sound about right?"

Sweat poured down the imam's face. Still unable to move his limbs, his eyes bulged with fear. "What's the matter, Uncle Baba?" Sharon added wryly, keeping her eyes on the road. "You should be overcome with joy. You're about to meet Allah, your lord and savior."

43

HAMPTON PULLED into the mortuary grounds and looked around. Aside from six black limousine hearses, there were only two vehicles in the parking lot. Lena was waiting for him and pointed to a spot next to her. "Sharon says everything went well. Is that right?" she asked as he stepped out of his truck.

"I used the drone to make sure everyone was inside before I blew the place. Seems like half the fire trucks in New York were sent to Staten Island."

Lena smiled. "Great job! It's all over the news. Already there's a rumor from an anonymous source that it was an accidental detonation involving a terrorist cell. Body parts everywhere, unexploded c-4 found at the scene, yadda, yadda..."

Hampton had a puzzled look on his face. "So soon?"

Lena smiled and pointed to herself. "You're looking at the anonymous source."

Ron pointed to the mortuary. "And this?"

Lena nodded and opened the door. "Unfinished business. You're welcome to watch, or if you're squeamish, you can drive back to Philly and return the rental truck. Sharon and I will go back to the Hay-Adams tonight...after a long, hot day at the office."

Feeling a little queasy, Hampton ignored Lena's attempt at morbid humor. As they entered the crematorium room, he noticed a temperature gauge on one of the ovens was climbing past 700º. Shackled with steel cuffs on top of a wooden gurney was a naked man with thick black hair from head to toe. His feet were no more than sixteen inches directly in front of the oven door.

Sharon rushed to Hampton, grabbing him in a firm hug. "You did it!" She pointed to her prisoner. "Meet Imam Mustafa Shabbah, the spiritual leader of al-Qaeda in America. Raising her voice to make sure her victim could hear, she added, "When the temperature reaches 1100º, he's gonna fry."

"Looks like a Neanderthal," Ron commented. Staring at Lena with distaste, he asked, "How did you find this place, let alone convince the owners to let you operate their oven? What do you know about cremation?"

Lena was reading the imam's medical file. "It's a long story, but my best friend Anne owned a funeral home in Florida. She showed me how to operate the chambers. They're kind of like pizza ovens. These modern ones are all automated. Anne also taught me what to do before and after a body is burned, and what to look out for before sliding one into the chamber. She had a lot of contacts in the industry. Her name and a hundred thousand in cash bought me this place for the day, no questions asked."

She paused to finish reading the medical chart. "I'm checking the imam's file to make sure he doesn't have a pacemaker or any radioactive cancer seeds in his body that could explode in the heat." Lena turned to Sharon. "Looks clean. He's ready for prime time."

Ron groaned. "How can you joke about this? It's so...barbaric!"

Lena looked at him sternly. "Honey, this is nothing compared to what my friends and I did to a couple of cannibals in the Ocala National Forest back in the seventies. We fed 'em to a nest of alligators..."

Hampton's eyeballs seemed to pop out of their sockets. "Jesus, woman," he interrupted. "Are you insane?"

"No more than you...Orkin Man," Lena shot back. "Sharon told me what you said. Hey, lighten up. We're on the same side."

Ron blushed and turned to go. "You got me, lady. Do what you came for. This just isn't my thing."

Sharon followed him out the door. "Lena is a good soul, Hamp. Sure she's crude, but she grew up hard and had to fight every step of the way for what she has. She's an American icon.

"The bottom line is no one will ever know what we did today. We'll never be able to talk about it and we'll get no thanks for it. You'll go back to your office in Philly and I'll disappear. But we saved our country from one more round of terror until a new batch of radicals tries to take us on. Let's go with that for now, okay?"

"I'm good with it if you are," Ron replied. Hugging her again, there were tears in his eyes. As he climbed in the F-150, he smiled. "Keep it together, boss. Remember the good times and I'll remember my friend, Papa Dough."

Sharon shook off her tears and sighed. "Drive carefully back to Philly, okay? I owe you more than I can ever repay. Please give Will my thanks. Tell him I'll be in touch."

Hampton had barely made it out of the parking lot when Lena signaled Sharon to return inside. "He's coming out of his paralysis. What do you want me to do?"

Sharon rushed into the cremation room to find the imam struggling against his shackles and roaring in outrage. "You cannot do this," Shabbah was screaming. "I am an American citizen and I have rights. Kidnapping an imam—I will have your heads for this. Release me at once."

"Shout all you want," Sharon answered, matching his volume. "This place is soundproof." She looked at the oven temperature—1150º.

"Here's a taste of what you're in for." Sharon stepped to the control panel and pushed OPEN DOOR. Like a blow torch, a blast of flames engulfed the imam's feet, incinerating the hair on both of his legs and setting both feet aflame.

Sharon matched his hysterical howls of pain with a scream of her own. Ignoring the searing temperature, she put her lips next to the imam's ear and shouted, "Now you know what my family felt, you piece of shit." She pushed another button and the wooden gurney slid quickly into the flames, immediately turning his body into a boiling mass.

Closing the chamber door, Sharon turned away, shaking like a scarecrow in a windstorm. Lena hurried to embrace her quivering friend. "It's over, baby. It's over. Go now. Let me do the rest. I'll be here for a few hours. Are you okay to drive?"

"I-I think so."

"Take your time. I'll meet you back at the Hay-Adams tonight. Have a few drinks. Hell, tell Cal I said to order you a bottle of your favorite poison on me and get stinking drunk. You deserve it. Now go." She gently pushed Sharon toward the door.

Mentally drained and physically exhausted, Sharon got into her car, started the engine and pulled out of the lot and into a nearby McDonalds drive-through. Ordering a large coffee, she downed a few gulps and started for D.C., her mind and body on automatic pilot.

Sharon would remember nothing of the three-hour trip. Over the past twenty-four hours, she had crossed a dangerous line from sanity into derangement.

Why didn't I die? Another few seconds and I would have died in Duncan's arms. She resolved there would be no more tears, only emptiness. *Before, I existed to live. From now on, I will live to exist. I'm one of them now—one of the damned.*

Inside the crematorium, Lena sat patiently watching the body disintegrate. With more than four hours to complete the process, she had plenty of time to count the money and read the notebooks Sharon had brought with the imam. There were ten thick stacks of hundred-dollar bills, each secured with a currency band marked "$10,000"—a total of $100,000, she estimated. Unimpressed with the amount, she picked up one of the notebooks. After reading the first few pages, Lena stood at attention and exclaimed, "Jesus, Mary and Joseph!"

DAY ELEVEN

44

HAVERTOWN, PENNSYLVANIA
FRIDAY, 10 A.M.

A FRUMPY BLONDE entered the offices of Summerfield, Patton, Bromfield and Hyde, Attorneys-at-Law and walked up to the receptionist. "I don't have an appointment," the woman stated. "I need to talk to Gloria Hyde."

The receptionist came back with a stock answer, "Ms. Hyde is busy right now. I'll be happy to leave her a message. May I ask what this is about?"

"I'm Sharon Richards."

"Excuse me, ma'am," the receptionist curtly replied. "I know Sharon Richards. You're not..."

"I'm in disguise, Darla," Sharon interrupted, taking off her wig. She fluffed her fake bodice and smiled. "Do you want me to take this off, too?"

Darla blushed. "Oh, Mrs. Richards. I'm so sorry. Guess you have to do that because of all the reporters, right?"

Sharon nodded. "Please tell Gloria I'm here. I'll wait if she's with another client."

Darla buzzed the intercom and announced the visitor. Gloria came immediately and ushered Sharon to her office. The attorney seemed anxious. "Where have you been? We've been trying to get in touch with you."

Sharon dodged the question. "I'm afraid I can't say. What's up?"

"What's up is your portfolio—way up," Gloria answered. "And I hope it's okay to be blunt..."

"Of course. After what I've been through these past few days, nothing will surprise me."

Gloria looked at Sharon critically. Her face was the same, but aside from the disguise, this was not the same vulnerable woman she had visited after the cruise ship disaster. There was a definite hardness about her as if she had suffered additional trauma.

Gloria continued, hoping that the new information wouldn't send Sharon over the edge. "Two days ago we received notice from the coroner's office. They have identified Duncan by his dental records as one of the cruise ship victims. We're having the certificate of death expedited."

Sharon seemed to take the news in stride without emotion. "What about the boys?"

"Nothing so far. According to you, Duncan was outside on the balcony. His body was easy to locate compared to those inside the ship, where you said the boys were. I'm sure their bodies will be found...eventually. DNA identification will take time." Gloria hesitated and put a hand on Sharon's arm. "God, I'm sorry. I must sound so uncaring."

"Don't feel that way, Gloria," Sharon replied, patting Gloria's hand. "I appreciate the candor. Believe me, I've shed enough tears these past few days to float an armada, but I'm over that now."

Gloria backed away, staring into Sharon's eyes. "I don't know if I could be as strong as you, under the circumstances."

Sharon looked away. *If only she knew…*

After a couple of seconds, she regained her composure. "Look, I'm here to catch up, both on my finances and to let you know what I intend to do. I need you to handle the arrangements for Duncan…and eventually the boys."

Gloria nodded. "Of course, anything you need, remember?"

"This is going to sound cold, but I don't want to be around for the last rites. I refuse to let the press make my loss into a circus. I want everything to be anonymous and quick— cremation and scatter the ashes in the ocean. Cost is no object, so do what you think is best. Just no ceremony or publicity, understand?"

Hyde had a confused look on her face. "Are you going on a trip?"

"Yes, I'll be out of the country for a while. That's another thing you need to keep confidential, Gloria. I'll be in touch from time to time, of course, but I need to get away."

"I understand, Sharon. We'll take care of everything." Gloria decided to change course. "Now, may I show you what the firm has done with your trust since the cruise ship tragedy?"

"You said 'your trust.' Is it officially in my name?"

"Yes, Duncan's body has been identified and the cause of death is confirmed. By the terms of his will and trust, as his wife and sole heir, you now own the assets."

Gloria turned to an office computer. "If you can give me a few minutes, I will print out a list of your current holdings." She punched a few keys and the printer started rolling out pages of documents.

Turning back to Sharon, she continued. "We've done nothing with the coin collection or real estate holdings, but we repositioned all equities to take advantage of the country's recent attacks and the subsequent worldwide market collapse."

Sharon nodded her head. "Good thinking. What's the bottom line?"

Gloria smiled. "Prior to the collapse, your total holdings, including real estate and the collection, was about $150 million. It's complicated, but at the start of the collapse, we sold all the stocks and bonds, using the proceeds to short the market and buy precious metal ETFs."

As she retrieved a page and presented it to Sharon, Gloria beamed with pride. "This is a summary of all your holdings as of today."

Sharon glanced at the series of numbers before looking at the totals. She began to sweat. Pointing to the last number, she asked, "Is this...really?"

"Yes," Gloria replied with an even wider smile. "Your net worth is slightly over $500 million. We've reaped the rewards of the country's atmosphere of fear and worldwide political instability. Mind you, this is a departure from our normal conservative approach to investing, but we felt that the conditions merited such a drastic change and we were proven right. I caution that your portfolio is in an extremely volatile position now and could change with any hint of returning stability."

Sharon's mind was in overdrive. "Let me ask you a couple of questions. Do I have the power to instruct you how to move forward with these assets? That is, can I tell you how I want to invest from here on?"

"Yes, of course. The firm's role is just an advisory one unless you decide to give us the power to make decisions on your behalf. While Duncan's life was still in question, of necessity we retained the power. But now, as sole heir you have complete control of these assets."

"Okay, here's the second question. What if I have knowledge of something that will likely cause the equity markets to reverse course and move sharply in a positive direction over the next day or two? Would that be considered 'insider trading?'"

Gloria looked puzzled but answered her question. "Not unless you're found to be responsible for or somehow associated with this market fluctuation. If I may ask, what knowledge do you have?"

Sharon paused, deep in thought. *I am the cause, but will I ever be identified?* She decided to go with gut instinct. "I can't divulge any details, but within the next two days, I have good reason to believe that the President of the United States is going to make such an announcement."

Gloria hesitated as well. *This woman is making me nervous.* "And what would you like us to do?"

"I know enough about your terminology to be dangerous, but here's what I'd like. Sell all the market shorts, as you call them, and invest the proceeds proportionately back into the prior equities, whatever that entails. Then I want you to sell eighty percent of the precious metals stocks and invest those proceeds in those same equities. Can you do this immediately without being too obvious?"

Gloria shook her head. Covering the firm's ass was her top priority, but she also had a fiduciary obligation to her client. "I can't guarantee anything," Gloria answered with a touch of frost, but if you insist, we'll initiate your requests at once."

Sharon hesitated. *If all goes well, I'll be out of this country within the next day or two.* "Transfer another million to my checking account. Keep the collection and real estate holdings intact and follow my instructions with the rest. As for my home in Havertown, please prepare a quitclaim deed and transfer ownership to Kenneth and Phyllis Schumacher, my next-door neighbors and good friends. The trust can pay the gift tax.

"Give me time to prepare all the paperwork," Gloria answered, ushering Sharon to the lobby. "You'll need to sign quite a few forms."

Two hours later, with all the paperwork signed, Sharon shook Gloria's hand. "I'm sorry I can't be more forthcoming at this time. I urge you to take my advice with the rest of your clients, but that's your firm's decision."

She abruptly sat again. "One more thing, Gloria. Please get me a blank piece of paper." She started writing in longhand.

To the law firm of Summerfield, Patton, Bromfield and Hyde: If in the future, any or all of my holdings is threatened with seizure by the federal government or any other entity, I direct your law firm permission to transfer the proceeds to as many offshore accounts as you deem appropriate. No matter what the outcome, I hold your firm harmless for any loss of principal incurred from this date forward.

Sharon Richards, trustee of the Duncan Richards Trust.

After signing and dating the page, Sharon hugged Gloria and walked toward the door. "Like Duncan, I trust you with my financial life. Please let everyone here know that I truly appreciate everything your law firm has done for us..." She paused to correct herself, "or should I say, me? I'll be in touch."

Gloria sat in her chair and stared at the hastily conceived document, befuddled and numb with worry. *Who is this mysterious woman and what trouble is she in?*

45

THE WHITE HOUSE
OVAL OFFICE
11 A.M.

"THANKS FOR making room in your schedule to see me, Liz," Lena said, hugging the president.

"My time is yours, Lena," Elizabeth Stanton replied with a smile, belying the absurdity of her remark. Gesturing for both of them to sit, she added, "I hope you came with good news."

"The best possible news," Lena replied. Over the next ten minutes, she related all but the gory details of the past two days, ending with, "If you wish, I'll be glad to work with the speech writers on your address to the nation."

The relief on Stanton's face was palpable. "So, I can tell the world that this terrorist cell has been eliminated and none of these bastards will come back to haunt us?"

"You can. Eliminated is a good word. It's important that we be no more specific than that."

"I am curious, though," the president added, "just between us, what did you do with the imam's body?"

"Let's just say, he's *'Blowin' in the Wind,'*" Lena answered with a straight face, referring to the popular 1962 Bob Dylan song.

The president nodded soberly and changed subjects. "Now, what can we do for this daring woman and her FBI friend she calls Hamp? The nation owes both of them a tremendous debt of gratitude."

"Last night I had a long talk with Mrs. Richards," Lena answered. "She was more than a little tipsy from the stress and some single malt Scotch—truth be known, that's my fault—but she is adamant that both her name and Hampton's be kept out of your address to the nation.

"Sharon has only two requests from you. First, that she be allowed to disappear. She intends to live in another country, retaining her U.S. citizenship, of course. And second, that you continue to have her back if any details or rumors of the operations are leaked to the media."

"Of course, she wishes to remain anonymous," the president replied. "That will be your job, to deflect and deny. Please tell this remarkable lady that whatever she wants, her grateful government will provide, including buying a residence of her choice in another country. It's the least I can do for an American patriot."

Lena shook her head and smiled. "That won't be necessary, Liz. Last night she told me about her husband's trust. Now that he's dead, she'll receive a considerable spousal inheritance, more than enough to purchase a residence anywhere in the world, as well as finance the lifestyle of her choice. She makes me look like a 'Little Sister of the Poor.'"

The president pursed her lips and nodded once for emphasis. "Good for her. Now, what can I do for Agent Hampton."

Lena pulled a letter from her purse. "Sharon wanted me to give you this. If you'll do what she asks for Ron, she wants to pay for it."

Stanton read the short letter. "Consider it done. I'll make sure it arrives at his office by Monday morning."

Next, Lena pulled out the imam's cash and the two notebooks from her large purse and handed everything over to the president. "Which brings me to the last and most important reason I've come today. When Sharon captured the imam, she also removed the contents of his safe. Besides this cash, she found these two ledger notebooks that contain information regarding a staggering amount of terrorist funding in offshore accounts. There are names, addresses and phone numbers of thirty-two international banks with corresponding contacts, codes, account numbers, passwords and amounts. I added up the total. It exceeds two billion dollars, enough funding to finance all the al-Qaeda terrorist operations around the world for years.

"This imam wasn't just a spiritual leader of an American splinter group of terrorists. He was a major player, possibly the most powerful financial coordinator for al-Qaeda affiliates in the world."

The president sat back, leafed through one of the books and whistled under her breath. "You're telling me this imam had the arrogance to leave these books in his office safe where anyone could steal them?"

"Sharon told me that he never left the mosque and guards patrolled the surrounding grounds nearly all the time. But, to answer your question, yes. He was that arrogant. Besides, think about it. Where else would he have kept the ledgers?

He didn't trust U.S. bank vaults, and it would be stupid to bury them. The imam had the gall to think our laws would provide protection for the mosque and shield his operation under the Freedom of Religion clause of the First Amendment."

President Stanton smiled, anticipating the answer to her question before she asked it. "Just what do you suggest I do with these books?"

Lena grinned back at her friend. "If you want my opinion, Madam President, I would enlist an army of CIA agents and use the internet to coordinate a worldwide simultaneous run on all these accounts. Strip the bastards of their financing and establish a fund to compensate the thousands of survivors and relatives of those who died in the attacks of the last ten days." She added with a wry smile, "If you want to add insult to injury, I've got one more suggestion for you..."

A moment later, Stanton roared with laughter. "My god, girl, that's pure genius! I want you at the press conference. You're in charge of delivering that bombshell. Meanwhile..." She punched the intercom to her secretary, "Madelyn, please buzz CIA Director Hank Collins over in Langley and have him come to the Oval Office immediately."

Turning to Lena, she added, "Now let's get you and my team of writers together. Make me a brief announcement for Monday's press conference. It's about time our country had something to cheer about!"

DAY FOURTEEN

46

FBI REGIONAL FIELD OFFICE
PHILADELPHIA
MONDAY, 11 A.M.

RESIDENT AGENT-IN-CHARGE Will Lambert looked up from his desk as Ron Hampton walked into the office. He motioned for Hampton to sit. "Well, how did it go?"

Ron shook his head. After a restless weekend at his apartment, he still felt drained, both physically and mentally. "Very well. You know I can't talk about it."

Lambert smiled. "Well, you must have done something right because this arrived about an hour ago." He handed Hampton an empty FedEx envelope, addressed to FBI RAIC William Lambert. "See the sender's name and return address?"

Hampton looked worried. "It's from the president. What does she want? Is it about me?"

Will chuckled and handed over an envelope addressed to Agent Ronald Hampton. Inside was handwritten letter over the Presidential Seal. "Check this out, Hot Shot. You've got friends in high places."

Dear Agent Hampton,

It has been brought to my attention that you have performed with exemplary distinction in the recent operation against the terrorist organization known as "al-Qaeda in America." As you know, the details of the operation must remain classified as well as your role in it, but in a separate enclosed letter, I have asked your RAIC Will Lambert to give you paid leave for a month to use as you wish. I hope that, on behalf of your country, in this small way I can convey the nation's utmost admiration for a job well done.

When the appropriate time comes, it will be my pleasure to acknowledge your brave actions and welcome you to the White House for dinner with me and my husband. Until then, please accept my most humble thanks.

Sincerely, Elizabeth Stanton

Ron looked up at his boss. "I don't know what to say."

"Don't say anything," Lambert replied, handing his agent another sealed envelope. "This was also inside the FedEx package. It's from Lena Mills."

Hampton accepted the envelope with a wordless nod. Inside was a note and another smaller envelope marked *To Ron*.

Dear Ron,

I'm sorry if we parted on acrimonious terms. Please pardon my bluntness. It's just the way I'm built. Sharon told me that you did a hell of a job. I'm sure she's right, and for that, you have my thanks.

She asked me to include another envelope from her. I've enclosed everything with the president's letter and mailed it to your boss. May we meet again in the future under more pleasant circumstances.

Sincerely, Lena

P.S. You're wrong. Ella Fitzgerald was the best jazz singer ever.

For the first time since he pushed the iPhone SEND button, Ron laughed.

"Care to share the humor?" Lambert asked.

"Sorry, boss. It's an inside joke between Lena and me. That woman is one feisty broad."

Lambert shook his head. "Okay. By request of the president, I'm ordering you to get lost for a month. Give your

Sharon my regards." He rose to smile and shake his agent's hand. "Now, take your ass-kissing letters and get out of here."

Ron left his boss in a cloud of euphoria. Sitting in his office, he stared at the president's letter, reading it over and over. After a while, he remembered to open Sharon's envelope and pulled out a note, a fancy travel brochure and two airline tickets.

> *Hamp,*
>
> *I hope I'm not being presumptuous, but I've taken the liberty of reserving a week at the Bird of Paradise, Anguilla for you and your Sharon. Duncan and I spent the best week of our lives there and I want you two to share that same experience.*
>
> *I've also checked with Sharon's school. That week is at the beginning of her summer break and shouldn't interfere with her teaching schedule. Of course, if you don't want to use this, please call the number on the brochure and cancel at least two days before your week commences.*
>
> *As for me, I'll be out of the country for a while looking for a suitable home, so if you need to reach me, leave a message on my cell.*

Your friend, Sharon

Ron's hands shook as he opened the brochure. A certified check for $500,000 dropped to the floor, followed immediately by the FBI agent's jaw.

47

**THE WHITE HOUSE
BRIEFING ROOM
2 P.M.**

PRESIDENT ELIZABETH STANTON stepped to the podium, followed by Lena Mills, who stood behind and off to the side. Because of the non-stop advance publicity over the weekend, this press conference was being televised nationally with links to many outlets around the world.

"Good afternoon. Before I make an announcement, I would like to introduce someone who has been out of the limelight for a few years, but whom most of you know well—Ms. Lena Mills."

Lena smiled as the press corps buzzed among themselves for a few seconds. "Ms. Mills has consented to be an occasional media liaison for me and America's Terrorist Task Force, so you will be seeing more of her as the need arises. When I'm done here today, Ms. Mills will make her own announcement.

"Now to the matter at hand. As your president, it is my sworn duty to protect the public. To that end, it is my pleasure to announce a piece of great news. The threat of future attacks by the terror cell calling itself al-Qaeda in America has been eliminated."

In a breach of press protocol, a round of applause erupted, followed by a number of raised hands. The president held up her arms. "Please, let me finish. For reasons of national security, and to keep any potential copycat groups guessing, neither I nor any member of my administration will be divulging details about the operation that achieved this goal. Although I want to assure the American public that this specific threat has been eliminated, it is imperative that we remain vigilant and prepared for any future domestic threats to our country and way of life. Unfortunately, it seems that we may be in for a generational war against radical Islam, at home and abroad. The same can be said about the ongoing threat of a global pandemic such as the ebola virus. For these reasons, I am instructing the National Guard and Border Control to do everything it takes to permanently lock down the borders with Mexico and Canada from future illegal immigration.

"Now I'll take a few questions before I turn the podium over to Ms. Mills." Over fifty hands shot up at once. The president pointed to a senior member of the press corps, NBC reporter Sandra Wiggins. "Sandy?"

The short, stocky grandmother was known for her skepticism, regardless of political bent. "Madam President, how can we be sure this latest threat of home-grown terrorism is eliminated if we don't have any details of the operation?"

"Sometimes the president has to weigh national security concerns against the public's right to know," Stanton answered. "The last thing we want to do is give away our playbook to those who would want to do us further harm. That's why the need for secrecy in this instance."

Buoyed with confidence, she looked further back in the room and gambled, pointing to Theodore Marcus, CNN's Chief Washington Correspondent, a fierce critic of her administration. "Ted?"

Marcus wasted no time with platitudes. Omitting her title, he addressed the president with scorn. "I have a reliable source who states that this *operation*, as you call it, was nothing more than an illegal assault on United States citizens without due process of law, resulting in the murders and/or disappearance of a Nobel Prize-winning physicist and a prominent imam, as well as over twenty other men. What do you have to say about this?"

Though Elizabeth Stanton remained outwardly calm, she was seething inside. Everyone was writing furiously. The room was silent, anticipating a presidential eruption. "Does your so-called reliable source have any proof of these allegations?" Stanton asked.

"He claims firsthand knowledge. That's all I can say," answered the reporter. "Any comments?"

"Yes, Ted. I'm up here talking about national security and you're asking me an inane and unsubstantiated question. Tell your source to put up or shut up." After taking three more questions about foreign policy matters and ignoring Marcus's persistently raised hand, she glanced at Lena as if to say, "They're all yours," and marched out of the room.

The fifty-plus press corps turned *en masse* to the CNN bureau chief and assailed him with howling protests. Lena watched the verbal melee with mixed emotions. *This reminds me of the good old days,* she thought and smiled. *Jack Gardner is the only one besides the president, Sharon and me with that information. Liz will want to crucify him.*

Lena took to the podium and stood there, saying nothing, letting the tongue-lashing play itself out. Senior correspondents remembered this blonde and popular fireball of past political dust-ups. Eager to witness her resurrection, they began to shush the younger reporters, anticipating that great theater was about to commence.

Finally, the room lapsed into silence. Lena opened her mouth to speak but was preempted by a cry from the back. "You da broad!" The room erupted in laughter and applause. Lena grinned. "Just like the old days," she commented, stepping beside the podium and bowing deeply. Returning to the bank of microphones, she glared at the CNN reporter and began, "Theodore Marcus, you were a pain-in-the-ass when I knew you years ago. I'm glad to see you haven't changed."

More laughter and finger-pointing toward Marcus, who blushed and grimaced. Lena waited again for silence. "Look, everyone, you have to admit, our country has been under unprecedented assault these past ten days—over twenty thousand deaths and counting, even more injured, riots in the streets and threats of more violence by a homegrown cabal of terrorists. The president came here to announce the first piece of good news since these assaults began. Let's give her some credit for doing her job.

"As you know," she continued, "in addition to these attacks, President Stanton has a pile of international conflicts to negotiate as well as security and economic matters here at home. Over the weekend, just the prospect of a positive announcement has created an upward surge in the markets today. I would bet they will skyrocket the rest of today and tomorrow after hearing the news I'm about to reveal."

Earnest shuffling could be heard throughout the room, as many reporters scrambled to place market orders on the internet. "I rest my case," Lena said, waving her arm across the room. What's the Michael Douglas line? 'Greed is good,' right?"

Embarrassed eyes refocused on her as she continued "As the president said, by necessity, the details of the operation must remain classified. I can, however, give you and the American public one piece of raw meat."

Lena paused to scan the audience of reporters. Everyone was sitting forward in rapt attention. "We have irrefutable evidence that the leader of this well-organized group calling itself al-Qaeda in America was an imam, who directed the attacks from his mosque. While I cannot reveal this person's name or the name of his mosque, I can tell you that he is a naturalized citizen of the United States. He must have been alerted of his impending arrest since he has disappeared." As she said the last sentence, the first two fingers of her right hand crossed behind her back.

A reporter from FOX News blurted out, "How can the president say the threat has been eliminated when the leader of the group remains at large?"

A number of arms went up. Lena cursed herself for being careless. She decided to ignore the question. "Please, let me finish. The good news is that we were able to confiscate the contents of this imam's safe. Besides a significant amount of cash, there were two ledger books that contained a list of offshore banks with account numbers, passwords, contacts, phone numbers, and most important, asset totals.

"It appears that this imam was a significant financial broker for the worldwide al-Qaeda network because the total cash in all the accounts exceeded two billion dollars."

A collective gasp went up throughout the room. "That's billion, with a B," she emphasized.

More arms raised. "Hold your horses," Lena insisted again, "I'm not done yet. Over the weekend, the president authorized a small army of CIA agents to strip these foreign accounts of their cash and have the proceeds wired to the U.S. Treasury. I'm happy to report that the cash was successfully transferred. As of now, all two billion plus of terrorist money is sitting in a separate account, safe and secure in the good ol' U.S. of A."

Lena held up her hands once more. "I have one more bit of information." She winked at the first row of reporters. "You're going to love this. The president has directed that this money will be allocated to the survivors and families of those killed in the six terrorist attacks. The fund will be called..." She paused for effect, "the al-Qaeda Apology Fund."

Watching the action from the presidential suite, Elizabeth Stanton smiled as she witnessed the loud standing ovation. Her husband shook his head in amazement. "I'm glad that woman is on your side. I've never seen someone toy with the press like that. You better hope she doesn't have presidential aspirations."

"Hon, that woman has more skeletons in her closet than the Roman catacombs. No way she'd want to subject herself to that kind of scrutiny."

Abruptly, the president's mood changed from pleasure to rage. Turning to her husband, she vowed, "I'm not sure how to do it, Ed, but somehow I'm going to crucify that asshole, Jack Gardner."

"Why not leave that to Lena?" Ed argued. "Your team has dealt a crippling financial blow to radical Islam and she just added insult to injury. The woman is diabolical and seems to relish a good fight."

Elizabeth Stanton hugged her husband and laughed. "Maybe I'll ask her. What say, my guru," she teased him, "should I create a new cabinet position—Secretary of Revenge?"

From his home in McLean, Virginia, Jack Gardner was watching the news conference with a different set of emotions. He had risen to power with the liberal lawyers and brilliant campaign strategists who had taken over D.C. in the previous administration.

Jack had virtually no experience in foreign affairs, but with a doctorate in political science from Harvard and a minor in ass-kissing, his credentials were good enough to be chosen as the former president's National Security Advisor.

Summarily dismissed by the current president, Elizabeth Stanton, Jack let his anger affect his thinking. Ignoring her threat of retribution, the day after he was fired he had contacted his favorite reporter, Theodore Marcus, and related what he had heard during the Oval Office conference with Lena Mills.

"I'm telling you, Ted, the president is planning to take out a group of U.S. citizens, vigilante style. One is a powerful imam in Brooklyn named Mustafa Shabbah, and another is a world-famous physicist and winner of a Nobel Prize, Dr. Muhammad Abu Mazra, who teaches at CUNY."

"This is political dynamite," Marcus had replied, furiously taking notes. "The woman is only a few months in office and already she's gone off the reservation. Do you have any proof of these allegations?"

Jack rose to his feet. "I was there when the president and that witch Lena Mills discussed their plans. It's gonna happen, Ted, mark my words!"

"Well, if it does, I'll raise your allegations. Without any evidence, though, that's all I can promise."

Two days later, newspapers, radio and TV stations throughout the country were headlining news of an early morning explosion in Staten Island. The New York Times shouted, *ANOTHER BOMB! AL-QAEDA MISFIRE? Preliminary reports of c-4 residue at the scene suggest that an unknown number of terrorists, possibly the "al-Qaeda in America" cell, were assembling crude bombs when one accidentally detonated, killing all in the immediate area.*

The following day, Saturday, three short notices appeared on the front page of the Times. *Influential Imam Disappears from Brooklyn Mosque; Nobel Prize-winning Physicist Missing; CUNY Physics Associate Professor Found Dead in Apartment.*

254

CNN Washington Bureau Chief Ted Marcus was at home expecting Gardner's call. "See, I told you the president was going on a vigilante killing spree," the former security advisor shouted. "What're you going to do about it?"

"There's a news conference scheduled for Monday at two. I'll bring it up, but again you have no proof of anything—just your word, Jack," Marcus cautioned. "Challenging the President of the United States is dicey at best with proof. Without any, you're asking for trouble."

From his home in Pennsylvania, Jack Gardner watched the news conference as the president and Lena Mills wiggled their way out of Ted Marcus's accusation. *Now the shit has hit the fan. The press will nip at their heels until the truth comes out,* he guessed.

He was wrong. Gardner's political career had been filled with bad decisions and ill-conceived notions. This mistake would be his undoing. The former security advisor had ignored the obvious—genuine relief felt by the American people. By a large majority, they only wanted their lives back and weren't concerned about the details.

Jack Gardner had let his bruised ego trump common sense and was about to suffer the worst possible political and social death by the Mistress of Retribution—Lena Mills.

DAY SIXTEEN

48

MCLEAN, VIRGINIA
WEDNESDAY, 9 P.M.

FOR THE PAST two days, Rodney Chambers had been observing the two-story house on Chain Bridge Road as well as its owner's habits. Researching Fairfax County newspaper articles and public records on his assigned subject, the private investigator learned that Jack Gardner was single, in his mid-fifties, a Harvard grad and a member of the exclusive Golf Club at Lansdowne, northwest of his home in McLean.

On Tuesday morning, Lena Mills had driven to Rodney's office and hired the thirty-two-year-old former computer programmer, now one of the most successful private investigators in the area. It was rumored but never proven that he moonlighted as a skilled burglar.

Lena reminded Chambers that Gardner was the president's recently fired National Security Advisor. "He's a tough cookie and his home will probably have a good security system," she said. "Think you can get inside without being noticed and do what I want?"

"Lady, I haven't yet come across a home with security I can't breach. I study the subject and locate all possible deterrents before I enter. Piece o' cake!" he boasted.

"I'm serious, Rodney," she warned, gripping his arm hard for emphasis. "I'm paying you a small fortune. Do not, under any circumstances, steal anything, leave prints or get caught on camera. Just find his passwords and do exactly what I say with his personal computer. Then get out and report to me, understand?"

Rodney's eyes lit up. "Hey, weren't you the broad—er—lady, on TV yesterday, jammin' with those White House press weenies?"

Lena was used to dealing with overconfident braggarts like Rodney. She went nose-to-nose with him and put on her most threatening look. "Yeah. I'm old enough to be your grandmother and I've got friends in high places. We'll kick your skinny ass to hell if you snitch on me, get it?" She pulled out a thick wad of hundreds from her handbag and counted out twenty-five. "Half now and the other half when you complete the job."

Rodney looked at the pile of money and laughed. "You got it, Grannie!"

Fast as lightning, Lena jammed a vise grip onto his privates, bringing Rodney to his knees. "Cross me and you'll be singing soprano for the Mormon Tabernacle Choir," she hissed. The arrogant investigator howled as she twisted her grip for emphasis. "And don't call me Grannie!"

Rodney had done his research. Using powerful binoculars, he had watched Gardner punch the codes for his gate and front door, disabling the house alarm system. *Stupid dolt,* the PI thought, *he uses the same numbers for both.* From the town's daily newspaper, he learned that his subject would be the guest of honor at a fund-raising event at his country club this evening, which meant he would likely be gone until at least midnight, downing cocktails and shaking hands with the locals.

Gardner's car exited the gate at seven-thirty. Waiting until nine for complete darkness, Rodney slipped on cotton gloves, walked up to the gate and punched in the numbers, repeating the code at the front door. Once inside, he checked each room carefully for surveillance cameras. To Rodney's relief, there appeared to be none.

Finding Gardner's home computer in the den was easy. The hard part would be to locate his list of passwords if it existed. Without it, he would have to be creative, since he only had Jack's date of birth, names of his parents and a few other references from the articles he had read.

Once again Rodney was in luck. Right on top of the first desk drawer he checked was the list of passwords. He was in.

Five minutes later, Rodney Chambers exited the house and grounds more excited than he went in. *This was the easiest fifty grand I'll ever make.*

Lena's cell phone rang at eleven p.m. She wasn't expecting to hear from Rodney until the next day. Swearing silently, she got out of bed, fearing the worst. *That bastard better not be in jail.*

"Who the hell is calling you at this hour?" asked Cal, rolling over on his side of the bed.

"I'll take it in the other room," she answered. "Go back to sleep."

Lena closed the bedroom door and answered the phone. "Who's this?" she demanded.

"Who do you think it is?"

"Cut the shit, Rodney. What's the problem? What happened?"

Rodney was in a euphoric mood and three shots of J&B down on a half-liter binge. "Ever'thing went smoother than a baby's bottom, Gran...oops, ma'am," he slurred.

"You're drunk. Just tell me, did you do what I asked with Gardner's computer?"

"Thas wha' I'm callin' 'bout. Didn' haf to. His rig's loaded with kiddie porn already. When do I get the res' o' my loot?"

"You better not be lying, Rodney. I'll hunt you down with a cattle prod."

Rodney sobered up immediately at the thought. "No, ma'am, as God is my witness, the dude is a certified perv!"

"You'll get paid once Gardner's arrested, which should be tomorrow morning. Now go home and sober up. On second thought, keep drinking. Maybe you'll die on the way home and I won't have to pay you. Good job and goodnight."

Lena clicked off and smiled. Her hunch was correct. Jack Gardner was his own worst enemy. She raised a fist. *Gotcha, you son-of-a-bitch!*

DAY SEVENTEEN

49

THE WHITE HOUSE
CABINET ROOM
THURSDAY, 6 A.M.

PRESIDENT ELIZABETH STANTON stood and held up the daily briefing, waving it in the air for the roomful of cabinet members to see. Lena Mills and her husband Cal sat in a back corner of the room. Cal sat stone-faced while Lena wondered why they had been included.

"Things are finally starting to go right, at least for the time being," Stanton began. "The equity markets are rebounding nicely, the riots in our streets have been quelled and Iran has backed off its threats of a nuclear attack on Israel. Accordingly, I've directed that our threat level be lowered to DEFCON 3.

"As you all know, along with Congress, we've given all domestic energy companies the green light to extract as much oil, natural gas and coal as possible, in keeping with strict safety and environmental regulations, of course. As a leading energy exporter, we're soon going to be able to underbid the Arabs and the rest of the Middle East at every turn. Let them choke on their oil.

"My promise to cut off aid to Mexico and all Central American countries yielded immediate results. According to the border patrol, within the span of only one week, illegal crossing attempts on our southern border have slowed to a trickle.

Stanton sat and sighed, signaling a mood change. "Finally, I want to alert you to something you will see on the news today. An hour ago, local Virginia police, assisted by a team of FBI agents, arrested former National Security Advisor Jack Gardner at his home and confiscated his computer, which reportedly contains several downloads of child pornography. Other than to say I'm shocked and saddened by this, I won't be making any other comments."

The president leaned back in her chair. "A lot has happened over the last couple of weeks. We must remain vigilant, but at least, we've served notice to all who would do our country harm that we won't be playing nice anymore. Let the lawyers, ACLU, and human rights activists scream. Let them threaten me with impeachment and challenge me in the courts. I will stand firm in my resolve to do whatever is necessary to protect our country from harm."

She paused for effect. "If any of you disagree with my procedures, I'll understand and accept your resignations. You are all patriots, no matter what your political leanings, and the country owes you a debt of gratitude. Contrary to the view of the previous administration, it's not important for the rest of the world to like us, but it's mandatory that the rest of the world respects our resolve."

The president pointed to the back of the room. "Finally, on behalf of a grateful country, I want to thank the lady in the back of this room. She has never been politically ambitious, yet ever since I met this remarkable woman, we have shared and worked toward the same goals—to follow the fundamental principles that the founders so eloquently included in our Constitution, and to protect the sovereignty of the strongest and most generous country this world has ever seen.

"You've all heard about Lena's exploits of the past, but none of you can know what she has done recently for her country, because most of it is, and will remain, classified. For that reason, the honor I'm about to bestow upon her will not be presented in public, but rather here in this room with you as the only witnesses.

"Lena has never sought compensation or accolades. Despite her many detractors, polls say she has the love and gratitude of the vast majority of Americans. She and her husband Cal Carpenter will be returning home to Florida tomorrow, but she has offered to be on call for me in the future. Who knows, I just may take her up on that. But for now..."

The president stood again and opened a small, flat box. "Lena and Cal, will you come over here and stand next to me?"

Looking bewildered, Lena grasped her husband's hand as walked to the president's side. The room buzzed with anticipation. Stanton pulled a bronze disk attached to a decorative blue ribbon from the box, placed the ribbon over Lena's head, and gave her a ten-second hug. "Don't even think of rejecting this, girlfriend," Stanton whispered in her ear, "I can think of no one who deserves it more than you, so shut up and deal with it."

Standing back, the president announced, "Lena Mills Carpenter, on behalf of a grateful nation, I am honored to present to you the Presidential Medal of Freedom for your lifetime of selfless contributions to the United States of America." She joined with everyone else in a standing ovation.

Cal hugged and kissed his wife while Lena's eyes welled with tears. "Did you know about this?" she asked her husband.

He simply grinned, stood back and joined the others in applause. When it finally died down, Cal was beaming with pride. "For the first time in her life," he announced, "my wife is speechless." Everyone broke out in laughter and came forward to congratulate the American icon.

On the drive back to Florida, Lena took the medal out of its box. "I've spoken in front of thousands and received more standing ovations than I can count. Nothing has ever meant more to me than this."

Cal was driving and answered, "I only wish my father could have met you. Hell, I wish I could have met *him*. Now you both have something in common."

Never one to miss the opportunity for a snarky jab at Lena, Claude responded from the back seat. "Your father won the Congressional Medal of Honor for saving lives on the battlefield."

Cal looked back and responded, "That may be, but more than once, Lena has saved the entire country."

Likewise, Chareen never missed an opportunity to jab at her husband. Elbowing Claude in the ribs, she added, "Yeah, put that in your pipe and smoke it!"

"Sweet cheeks, you know I don't smoke," Claude replied.

"Babycakes," she cooed suggestively, "you do in bed. You just never looked."

Lena shrieked in delight and high-fived Chareen. Cal chuckled so hard he had a coughing fit and almost drove off the road. After the laughter died down, Lena asked, "So, what do y'all think of our president?"

"Teddy Roosevelt said it best," Cal answered. "'Speak softly and carry a big stick.'"

"Except Liz doesn't speak softly," argued Lena.

Claude chimed in. "But she does have a big..."

"Not as big as yours," Chareen interrupted, causing another round of hysterical laughter. Lena turned to high-five her again. Claude was blushing, silenced by the two indomitable women he loved more than life itself.

Cal pulled into the nearest rest stop. "That's it. I can't drive with George Burns and Gracie Allen in the car."

Ten minutes later, when Lena took the driver's seat, everyone was still laughing.

EPILOGUE

PHILADELPHIA, PENNSYLVANIA
SIX MONTHS LATER

WILL LAMBERT pulled his Honda Accord into a reserved space that came with his new retirement digs, a country club condo. Sweaty after eighteen holes, he had downed the obligatory beer with his golfing buddies in record time and begged off the usual poker game, opting instead for a hot shower at home and the Stouffer's frozen entrée that had been eating at his mind since the par three twelfth.

Retrieving his mail, Will entered the apartment, popped the dinner into his microwave and set it for seven minutes on high. He shucked off his clothes and, for the second time this day, showered and shaved. If he didn't have the second date tonight with his latest prospect, Penélope—*what was her last name?*—he would have skipped the latter, but the odds were better than even for a roll in the hay with the sexy Latin cougar, and he didn't want to spoil the mood with a prickly face.

Will sat back in his easy chair to consume the gooey tuna casserole. He had retired three months ago and settled into a routine, something he had been anticipating for years. But the change had been abrupt and merciless—from an active, exciting thirty-year career of fighting crime, to a meaningless

271

life of golf, watching TV and an occasional romp with a member of the opposite sex.

Most were widows looking to snare another husband. Penélope was the latest and, so far, his greatest challenge. With a thoroughbred body and stiletto temper, the fifty-something vixen had put two spouses in the grave and was trolling for a third. Will relished the challenge, if only as an antidote to his boredom.

Lambert's last divorce had drained his savings and would continue to cut in half his monthly retirement income until he died. Over the last twenty years, Debbie had let herself go, and the prospects of her re-marrying were in direct contrast to her bloated figure—slim. At least, neither of his exes had wanted a family, so there were no children to worry about.

His golf buddies had plenty of advice for their newest member. "Travel, write a book, take up a hobby like stamp collecting, volunteer at a local charity. That's what we do and we're happy." Looking into their eyes, Will knew they were fooling themselves. In truth, every one of them had surrendered to a dull, dispassionate existence that would eventually end in an ignominious passing.

Bottom line—after only three months, Will Lambert was sick of retirement. Disgusted with himself, he threw the rest of his food in the trash and grabbed the mail, expecting to see the usual pieces of junk and a bill or two. Under a flyer hawking a trade-in deal on a new car was a business-sized, hand-written envelope with two strange and colorful stamps attached. He found it odd that there was no return address on the front or back. The envelope was a bit bulky and the style of writing seemed vaguely familiar, but he couldn't place it.

Tearing through the top with his finger, Will removed a letter and a book of airline tickets. *What the hell...?* He put the tickets aside and concentrated on the letter.

> *Dear Will,*
>
> *I apologize for not calling or writing these past six months. After all the excitement, I just wanted to get away from my past and let the grieving process play out. After seeing where I am living now, you'll doubtless agree that I have at least accomplished my first objective.*
>
> *Hamp told me you've been retired for three months and have settled into a much-deserved life of leisure. The last thing I want is to intrude upon your new lifestyle, so if the rest of this letter is presumptive in any way, just discard it and I'll be content to remember you with fondness.*
>
> *Will, I've had some time to mourn the loss of my family and I've concluded that life must go on. Unless I completely misread you, when we worked together all those years, I sensed your attraction to me on more than a professional level. I felt the same toward you, but my marriage and family necessarily forbade any expression of these feelings.*

Now that things have changed, I'm taking a chance that my instincts were right. If for no other reason than you want to get away for a short time, I have enclosed with this letter open-ended first class tickets and transfers that will bring you to my new home in St. Barts.

Ron is here with his wife. Did you know he married last month? She is also named Sharon, which leads to some confusion, but I won't go into that now.

At any rate, I would love to see you again and I hope the feeling is mutual. All I ask is that you call, send me an e-mail or write a reply to this letter to let me know if and when you're coming. I'll take care of the rest.

Hamp has a message for you on the back. He says it's personal, so I won't read it.

With my warmest regards, Sharon

Below her signature was a phone number and e-mail address.

Excited and curious, Will turned over the letter.

Boss,

I also apologize for not communicating these past months, but things have been hectic and a bit dicey with Sharon (Richards, that is). She made me a generous offer to give up my career with the FBI and move with my wife to her compound here in St. Barts.

Sharon is stubborn and refuses to ask for your help, so I will. A high-level Islamic cleric has issued a death fatwa against Lena Mills. I'm afraid that may also apply to Sharon. Until and unless we see you, I can't go into details.

At any rate, I hope you can tear yourself away from the "good life" in retirement and take a few days to see how the one percent live here in the Eastern Caribbean. You won't regret the experience.

Best, Hamp

Will read the front and back of the letter again twice to digest the scenario. *Sharon's on a remote Caribbean island with Hamp and his new wife; they all live in a "compound," whatever that means; Sharon wants to see me and may be in trouble.*

His decision was immediate. Grabbing his cell phone, Will punched in Penélope's number and canceled this evening's date, explaining sheepishly that his latest blood test for STDs had come back positive.

After listening to her expletive-filled response in Spanish, he disconnected. Giving himself a few seconds to stop laughing, he dialed Sharon's number in St. Barts, more excited than he'd been in years.

TWO DAYS LATER

"LADIES AND GENTLEMEN, welcome to Saint Barts," the lone steward announced as the nine-seat Cessna pulled to stop at the Gustaf III Airport. "It's three-forty p.m. Atlantic Standard Time, the temperature is twenty-six degrees Celsius, or seventy-nine degrees Fahrenheit. The sun is out and the wonderful island of St. Barts is waiting to show you the time of your life."

Will Lambert looked out his small window and saw Hamp, a woman who had to be his wife and Sharon shading their eyes and waiting patiently for him to disembark.

Lambert's flight had left JFK International about nine a.m. and arrived at Julianna Airport in Dutch St. Maarten, where he had boarded the commuter plane for the short hop to St. Barts. All the way here he wondered, *Why would Sharon move to this remote island? Guess I'm about to find out.*

Hamp greeted him with a hearty handshake. "Welcome to paradise, boss. I'd like you to meet my wife, Sharon." A tall, slender beauty stepped forward and hugged Will. "I'm so happy to meet you, Mr. Lambert. Ronald has told me so much about you."

Turning to Hampton, Will smiled. "She's beautiful...*and* polite," he teased. Pointing to his former agent, he added sarcastically, "unlike some people I know...*Ronald.*" Hamp blushed while his wife giggled.

The other Sharon broke in with a sharp elbow to Hamp's ribs. "Hey, I hate to break up this love fest, but what am I,

277

chopped liver?" She threw her arms around Will and embraced him fiercely. "I could never do this at the office."

Temporarily thrown off balance, Will returned her hug with equal gusto. "I thought I'd lost touch with you forever. It's been over six months. How are you holding up?" he murmured in her ear.

Refusing to let go, she sighed. "Fine, especially now that you're here." There was a hint of desperation in her voice that belied her answer.

Finally, she released him and both stood apart to observe each other. Smiling widely, Sharon corralled her emotions. "Thanks for coming. You're looking great. Retirement definitely agrees with you."

"You've never looked better," he replied. *She's always been fit and sexy, but there's something different about her that wasn't there before.* "I've never been so glad to get anyone's letter. Retirement is boring the hell out of me."

"Well, all that's about to change," Hampton broke in. He was holding two bags. "These all you got?"

"Yep. I travel light."

Sharon marched toward the small terminal building. "Well, let's get you through customs and on the road."

Like many Caribbean islands, Saint Barthelemy has few straight roads. They either surround or climb a series of volcanic hills covered in lush tropical vegetation. Will had been to some of the islands years ago on cruises he had taken with his former wives, but he had never seen more stunning vistas as they climbed toward the interior.

Hamp was sitting in the back seat of Sharon's Jeep Wrangler with his wife. Watching his former boss taking in

278

the scenery, he leaned forward and commented, "We're not in Kansas anymore. Wait 'til you see where we're going. It's Oz on steroids."

Will silently nodded his head in agreement.

"Everyone calm down," Sharon ordered. "The poor guy's gonna think we've got some kind of goofy island disease."

Lambert broke from his sight-seeing and turned to look back at Hamp. "Why didn't you let me know you were getting married? Did you have a fancy wedding? I would have come bearing gifts."

Hamp looked guilty. "I think he'd rather hear it from you, Sher," he goaded his wife.

Sharon Richards stayed silent. She had enough to do navigating the switchbacks and hairpin turns.

"First, let's get this Sharon stuff straight," the brown-skinned beauty began. "Call me Sher and Sharon is Sharon. Got it?""

"Yes, ma'am," Will responded obediently. "That's a relief," he added in jest.

"Well, to answer your question, my funny man here kidnapped me to Anguilla, a nearby island, where he had a week to apply his full court press. I'm just a poor Philly schoolteacher who's never been west of the Mississippi, let alone to some exotic paradise. I fell in love with the culture and let the Hampster ravage me, but put him off on the marriage thing. Then, a few weeks later, he says he's moving to St. Barts to work for Sharon, and she has secured me a job teaching at a local school here if I want it.

"I minored in French in college. Nearly everyone here speaks both French and English." She threw her arms around her husband, planted a big kiss on his surprised lips and giggled. "What's a girl to do? I said yes."

Will couldn't resist. "Hampster? He looks more like a gerbil." Ron blushed while Sharon laughed. "By now," Will added, "you know he's a handful, but it sounds like you're very happy. Congratulations to you both."

Rounding one more corner, Sharon took a right and drove up to an imposing iron gate, surrounded by a double twelve-foot-high fence with barbed wire at the top. "It's electrified," she explained, clicking a remote attached to the driver-side visor. "Anyone trying to scale these two babies will get zapped and hung out to dry."

As the gate opened, Will's jaw dropped. A small village of modern concrete and glass structures, all linked by a giant, meandering swimming pool, spread out before him. "My god, woman, you own all of this?" he gushed.

Sharon nodded and smiled, letting the scene speak for itself. Hamp couldn't resist. "Boss, welcome to Chez Richard," he announced, using the French inflection *Re-shard*. "It's paradise with an attitude."

Pulling up to the largest villa, Sharon parked the Wrangler. "This compound was built by a Mexican drug lord who has long since died of unnatural causes. I'll explain everything later. Let's get you moved into one of these villas. Your choice, except those two." She pointed to the two buildings farthest from the main house. "One is the lovebirds' nest, and my personal chef lives in the other.

"Each one has a marvelous view," she continued, oblivious to Will's look of astonishment. "Which one floats your boat?"

"I...don't..." he babbled.

"Good. That's it, then," Sharon stated matter-of-factly. "You'll room with me. Let's get you settled and later I'll introduce you to my personal chef."

Hamp and Sher gave each other a knowing grin and walked off toward their villa. Will followed Sharon into the main house, not believing what he was seeing...or hearing. *"Personal* chef?"

She laughed, all but ignoring his question. "Yes, and I've got the perfect welcoming supper planned for you. I seem to remember that you like fish." She waited for him to nod yes. "The chef makes a killer Caribbean meal using a local triggerfish called 'old wife' by the natives. Sounds weird, but I guarantee you'll think you've died and gone to heaven."

Will's eyes were wide with wonder. "I'm already in heaven." Her open-air living room was a symphony of glass, polished chrome and onyx. A wide balcony overlooked a tranquil bay far below. "I...can't...believe this," he stammered. "This had to cost you..."

Sharon stepped in front of him and held a finger to his lips. "Rule number one. We never talk about my money." She took his hands in hers and stared at Will with a look that made him both hard and soft all over. "Rule number two," she murmured provocatively. "Kissing is encouraged."

"I like your rules," he replied, taking her in his arms and whispering in her ear. "Now show me the bedroom. Give me time to shave and shower and we'll negotiate rule number three."

Fifteen minutes later, Will emerged from the bathroom, wearing only a bath towel wrapped around his waist. Sharon had also freshened and changed into a sheer turquoise kimono. "You look spectacular," he commented, stunned by her sultry beauty. "That costume would never do at the office."

Sharon laughed and pointed to his growing bulge under the towel. "Neither would yours."

In one swift motion, she dropped the kimono. Sauntering in the nude toward him, she added, "You were saying something about rule number three?"

Will let his towel drop to the floor and took her in his arms. "Screw the rules," he growled.

Two hours later, Will and Sharon emerged from the bedroom, clothed but exhausted. An elderly, brown-skinned man with snow-white hair was waiting patiently in the kitchen. Sharon did the honors. "Will, this is Alphonse, the best kept secret chef in the world."

Alphonse bowed and smiled with a mouthful of shiny white teeth. "Missy still want old wife—for two tonight?" he asked.

"Yes, and surprise us with the extras, okay? We'll take supper on the balcony," Sharon answered. Guiding Will by the hand toward her fully stocked wine cooler, she commented, "I keep everything at fifty-six degrees Fahrenheit, what the French consider cave- or room-temperature."

Will nodded his head. "Yes, I know."

Sharon asked, "What's your pleasure tonight? Pick any one of these."

"Nothing in a bottle could compete with the pleasure of the last two hours," he replied, kissing her again. "But if you insist..." He surveyed the selection and whistled. "I'm not an expert, but I do know something about French vintages. Many of these are quite rare. He pointed at one bottle and whistled under his breath. *"Le Montrachet '87*—from Burgundy. Some consider this the best dry white in the world."

"I'm not an expert either, but I know what I like. Keep looking, monsieur," Sharon teased, pointing to another bottle labeled *1989 Les Clos Grand Cru*.

"My god!" he gasped. "A 'Comet Year' Les Clos! This is supposed to be impossible to buy at any cost. How did you find it?"

"I didn't, but I happened across Harrison Ford in town. Many famous people either live or visit here, and he gave me the name and contact information of a Frenchman known as the 'Sommelier to the Stars.' According to the Hollywood elites, this man can get just about anything...for a price. He found everything you see here."

Will answered, "Let's try the *Montrachet*. It would be sacrilege to open the *Les Clos*."

Sharon signaled to Alphonse, opened the door and placed the preferred bottle on the cooler floor. "We'll have this with supper," she announced. "Please open it ten minutes before serving the main course...to let it breathe, okay?"

Taking Will's hand, she walked him toward the balcony. "I had no idea you were this knowledgeable about wine, let alone such a romantic, Will Lambert. All those years we worked together...we've got a lot to learn about each other."

"And I had no idea you would be such a tiger in the sack," he replied. Seeing the hurt look on her face, he quickly backtracked and took her in his arms. "I'm sorry. That was crude and uncalled for."

"That's not why I'm emotional, Will. It's just that phrase. It brings back a bad memory. And I haven't made..." She omitted the word, "since Duncan died." Tears were in her eyes as she sat back in a full-length lounge chair, gesturing for him to do the same on one next to hers.

"You have to understand that Duncan and I had known each other since grade school. We went steady in high school. Why I was attracted to the self-centered pain-in-the-ass, I'll never know. We were definitely opposites. And yet he was a good father to his children and a faithful husband to me.

"I scolded him, even left him, when he went too far with that ridiculous scheme to catch the hit man. But it all worked out, we made up and he was a hero. You know all about that, but what you don't know is..." She began crying. "I really loved him...and now...he and my precious boys...are gone."

Will opened his mouth to speak, but Sharon shook off her tears and held up a hand. "Let me vent, okay? I need to get things off my chest, and that's your price of admission."

She looked at him. "You don't have to hear this. You can pack up and leave with no hard feelings. But I need you, Will. You're the only person I can trust with what's inside of me, the only person that can keep my top-secret information confidential."

He reached out and took her hand. "Of course. You know me well enough that I'm not in this for a quick fling. I'm in for the duration."

Sharon squeezed his hand gratefully. Will thought it was time to change the subject. "On the back of your letter, Hamp wrote something about a 'death fatwa' against Lena Mills. Does that have anything to do with your top-secret information?"

Sharon nodded. "This is going to take a while..."

After a luxurious swim in the pool and over a spectacular moonlit supper, Sharon told Will about Duncan's inheritance and how the law firm trustees used the extremely volatile market conditions to multiply the assets over the past year. Leaving nothing out, she related the events of the cruise ship disaster through her two revenge assassinations. "Let me ask you a question," she said at the conclusion of her story. "Have you ever killed someone up close and personal?"

He nodded. "I was trained as a sniper."

"So was I," she replied, "but there's a world of difference between killing someone from a distance versus face-to-face. I don't care how much the person deserves to die. Doing it that way takes away a part of your humanity." Sharon looked up at the star-filled sky and sighed. "And I've done it twice."

Will patted his lounge chair. "Come here...beside me."

Sharon curled up against his strong body and continued. "About two weeks ago, I got a call from the president's personal secretary, Madelyn Forsyth. It seems that a powerful mullah not only took offense that we captured over two billion from al-Qaeda offshore accounts and allocated it to the victims of the attacks, but went ballistic over Lena's idea of naming the reparations the 'al-Qaeda Apology Fund.' The mullah calls it an 'unforgivable offense to Allah and all of Islam.'"

Will chuckled. "I never met the lady, but Lena Mills is certainly a piece of work. Good for her!"

"Lena is used to threats, having survived two assassination attempts," Sharon continued. "She has her husband and friends, as well as the means to hire a small army of security personnel if she needs to. I'm not worried about her, but this is all new to me."

She sat up and turned to face Will. "Before he was fired by the president and arrested for possession of child pornography, Jack Gardner, the former National Security Advisor, let it be known that an unknown woman was responsible for Imam Shabbah's disappearance as well as finding his ledger of offshore bank deposits. Gardner was in on the meeting with the president and Lena when the recorded evidence was played and all of this was discussed. The press is on a tear, and it's only a matter of time before my name is leaked as this mystery woman."

Will growled, "That sick bastard! I hope he gets what he deserves in prison."

"So there you have it," Sharon ended with a sigh. "You're up-to-date now. I hired Hamp to help protect me here in my sanctuary. I never go anywhere on the island without him. He's already installed over thirty surveillance cameras with silent alarms around the perimeter of the compound, including some beside the stairs down to the beach. He's electrified the fence and is working on other measures to defeat an assault by air."

"Whose idea was it to write the letter to me?" Will asked.

"Hamp thinks it was his idea and that he talked me into doing it. I'm fine with that," she added. "I've missed you terribly, but I wasn't sure if you felt the same…" She glanced at his bulge and smiled, "until our little session earlier.

"Anyway, we need another man with your experience and a strong body around here. Even though I'm surrounded by all this luxury, I feel like an animal trapped in a cage. So here's my offer."

Sharon swung her leg over and straddled him. "Name your price and I'll double it. Free room and board, and the fringe benefits will be quite…generous. But only if you think I'm worth it," she added with a lingering kiss, grinding her hips onto his lap.

Under a full moon surrounded by more stars than he had ever seen, Will Lambert groaned.

"You had me at rule number two."

ACKNOWLEDGMENTS

The author acknowledges the trademark status and the following trademark owners mentioned in this work of fiction (not necessarily in order of appearance):

Boeing; Febreze; American Physics Society; Nobel Prize; Yellow Pages; American Numismatic Association (ANA); *The Late Show with David Letterman*; Apple; Toshiba; Range Rover; Jacuzzi; Qosimo; *Star Trek*; Fox News; Transamerica; Willis Tower; Capital Health Medical Center; Super 8 Motel; GMC; *U.S. News & World Report*; Bayer; Hay-Adams Hotel; Sysco; Caesar's Palace; Mall of America; Fontainebleau Resort; Monocle Restaurant; *Mahler's Ninth Symphony*; *William Tell Overture*; *The Lone Ranger*; Empire Room; Walmart; Target; c-4; Duct tape; Kleenex; *CSI*; Dove; Orkin; Dragonfly; Styrofoam; *Dr. Strangelove*; Montessori; Ford; *Blowin' in the Wind*; FedEx; Bird of Paradise Resort; Golf Club at Lansdowne; Honda; Oz; Le Montrachet; Les Clos.

All characters in this novel are fictional, except for the living or deceased persons listed below (not necessarily in order of appearance):

FBI Director Thomas Mueller; Omar Abdel Rahman; Francis Albert Sinatra; Osama bin Laden; King Abdullah; Dylan Thomas; Brian Williams; Margaret Thatcher; Bill Withers; President Bush; Abraham Lincoln; Timothy McVeigh; Michael Fortier; Terry Nichols; Gary Cooper; Charlton Heston;

Mubarak; Arafat; Abu Abdul Rahman a-Muhair; Ravi Shankar; Bob Dylan; Michael Douglas; George Burns; Gracie Allen.

***

I wish to acknowledge the assistance of two longtime friends, CAPTAIN JAMES HINSDALE and his wife SUSAN. Jim is a retired pilot, formerly with Eastern Airlines and Gulf Air. His guidance concerning the protocol of airline departure procedures was invaluable to the opening chapters of this book.

Sue Hinsdale is a former flight attendant and former owner of a retail wine shop. She gave me the names of the two rare wines featured in the Epilogue.

Jim also referred me to CAPTAIN DAVID CRAWFORD, a pilot and safety engineer with Gulfstream Aerospace. David provided information about the cockpit layout on the Boeing 777.

SUSAN WESTEN is another longtime friend. A current Delta Airlines employee, she provided the airplane cabin cleaning protocol that opens the story.

As with my other books, I am once again indebted to MARSHA BUTLER, my editor. She continues to bring her spot-on assessment of my work, as well as her unique and critical line and copy editing skills. Her role as "bad cop" to my "good cop" friends and family members makes for a much improved final product.

My daughters LAURA and MARY, and grandchildren ALLEN and CAITLYN, who give me the inspiration to keep writing, as well keep me up-to-date on the current vernacular whenever I lapse into outdated "geezer" terminology.

And, of course, CATHY—my wife of 45 years—who lends a critical but loving eye to my work and kicks my behind when I take too many naps.

THE AUTHOR HOPES YOU ENJOYED
AMERAGEDDON AND WELCOMES BOTH
POSITIVE AND NEGATIVE FEEDBACK. PLEASE
VISIT THE AMAZON BOOKSITE FOR THIS TITLE
AND SCROLL DOWN TO:

"LEAVE A CUSTOMER REVIEW."

"Puppy Breath" – Ethel England 2006

DAVID CARL MIELKE, author of the award-winning novels of the
LENA MILLS TRILOGY and *NICKELODIUM*, lives outside of Mount
Dora, Florida at One Mielke Way—home of One Diabetic Grandpa,
One Sweet Grandma, Two Candy-assed Dogs and One Sour Puss.
In addition to visits from family and friends who come for snickers
and snacks and such, he whiles away his remaining years with

hobbies and frequent naps. Strapping on a suicide laptop, he commits jihad on the English language, hoping to earn his seventy-two virgins—not that he would know what to do with them. Actually, the thought scares the hell out of him.

THE LENA MILLS TRILOGY

Book 1

MYSTIC SISTERS

OPPOSITES IN LIFE –
SOULMATES FOR ETERNITY

FROM EARLY CHILDHOOD, **LENA MILLS** develops a steely determination for retribution. Empowered with the face of an angel, a drop-dead gorgeous body and a cunning mind, she rips through adversity like an avenging tornado, leaving a trail of stunned antagonists and devastation in her wake.

Raised in a mortuary, **ANNE HENDERSON** learns at an early age that she has the power of a medium. A loner with the ability to communicate with live animals and dead people, she ponders the meaning of life until meeting and befriending her polar opposite, Lena Mills.

Lena and Anne discover they have one thing in common: both have bedded Congressman **WINTHROP ROCKLEDGE STEDMAN, III**—a randy, rising star in Florida politics. Payback is Hell for the libidinous letch as both women plot embarrassing retribution. **(Think: Thelma and Louise meet Bill Clinton.)**

Hold on to your sides as you wend your way through three decades of small town Central Florida, replete with quarreling townsfolk, a no-nonsense sheriff with a legendary ancestor, Cubano hit men, exotic dancers, a haunted house and a former Ziegfeld Follies girl, who still high kicks at age

80. Stir in Dracula, a well-hung skunk, and one nasty alligator named "Ol' Clyde" and you've got a recipe for laugh-out-loud mayhem.

Book 2

A NATION BEST SERVED HOT

RESCUED NEAR DEATH after months of torture by a demented Mexican drug lord, **EL GATO,** DEA agent **TRACY HENDERSON** lives for revenge but finds the greatest enemy lurks within her own mind. Itinerant gambler **JERRY CALVIN** is also on the run from El Gato over a card game gone wrong and a botched shipment of cocaine. Using his money and her skills, Jerry and Tracy join to plot a daring counterattack but find their love for each other gets in the way.

Former exotic dancer **LENA MILLS**—Tracy's adopted aunt— is engaged to Florida Governor **WIN STEDMAN,** only to lose him on their wedding night to a massive heart attack. Outspoken and eloquent, Lena uses her rising popularity and newly discovered ability to read minds and forecast the future to wage a mystically mandated war against corrupt politicians.

In this sequel to **A DISH BEST SERVED COLD,** ride a roller-coaster adventure of raw humor, retribution, and the triumph of the human spirit—as Lena, Tracy, and Jerry team up with sassy media magnet **MELONY MAJOR** to chase crooked congressmen from office and turn Washington on its ear.

Paraphrasing John Paul Jones:

THEY HAVE JUST BEGUN TO FIGHT!

Book 3

EXECUTIVE DECEIT

LENA MILLS THWARTS assassination attempts, disrupts two Senate confirmation hearings, deposes the President of the United States, finds the love of her life and brings the nation to the brink of polarized anarchy!

Which begs the question:

WILL OUR COUNTRY SURVIVE LENA MILLS?

ALSO Book 1 of the
<u>SHARON RICHARDS SAGA</u>
NICKELODIUM

DESIGNATED *"ONE OF THE BEST NOVELS OF 2014"*
BY THE FLORIDA AUTHORS AND PUBLISHERS
ASSOCIATION

IN THE ATTIC of an old Philadelphia home, estate salvager **DUNCAN RICHARDS** discovers a box of rare 1913 Liberty-head nickels, the most celebrated coins in U.S. history. While researching their origin, he senses a mysterious connection to **FLORENCE WYCHE**, a beautiful Philadelphia socialite, and her unsolved murder a hundred years earlier. Duncan auctions off one of the nickels for millions of dollars, while keeping the rest a secret. After the auction he produces another coin, prompting an outcry from collectors and threats to his life. When his brother is murdered, Duncan must take drastic measures to protect himself and his family.

Follow the intriguing twists and turns of *NICKELODIUM*—a story based on historical fact—as Duncan unravels the links between two generations of flawed characters separated by a century of questionable heritage. The surprise ending will leave you smiling and wanting more!

All of the author's works are available with Amazon in both Kindle and Paperback formats. Please check out the author's *KICK ASS* website:

www.davidcarlmielke.com

P.O. BOX 686
SORRENTO, FL 32776

www.ingramcontent.com/pod-product-compliance
Lightning Source LLC
Chambersburg PA
CBHW070306260626
47160CB00003B/740